"This small, exquisite book is a personal invitation to a day at Claude Monet's country house....Figes has adapted Monet's Impressionist technique to the novel, her touch as strong and delicate as his...."

Los Angeles Times

"GLOWS WITH THE BEAUTY, THE MIRACLE OF BEING ALIVE...We don't really need to know it is Monet; it is enough to see into the mind of an artist, painting portraits of life itself even while he is in its midst, surrounded, overwhelmed by it, by the riotous flowers, by the loves and griefs and flitting concerns of the people around him, by the evanescent light that bathes them. And light...is what this book is about: the moment illumined, the precious quicksilver instant that is the stuff of our existence, and the heroic madness of the artist who tries to capture it."

The Washington Post

L I G H T

E V A   F I G E S

BALLANTINE BOOKS • NEW YORK

Library of Congress Catalog Card Number: 83-42819

ISBN 0-345-31898-6

This edition published by arrangement with Pantheon Books

Manufactured in the United States of America

First Ballantine Books Edition: October 1984

One

The sky was still dark when he opened his eyes and saw it through
the uncurtained window. He was upright within seconds,
out of bed and had opened the window to study the
signs. It looked good to him, the dark just beginning to
fade slightly, midnight blueblack growing grey and misty,
through which he could make out the last light of a dying
star. It looked good to him, a calm pre-dawn hush without a breath of wind, and not a shadow of cloud in the
high clear sky. He took a deep breath of air, heavy with
night scents and dew on earth and foliage. His appetite

1

for the day thoroughly aroused, his elated mood turned to energy, and he was into his dressing room, into the cold bath which set his skin tingling, humming an unknown tune under his breath.

He dressed hurriedly and came back into the bedroom. I'm even ahead of the birds, he thought, standing at the open window one last time, leaning forward with his hands on the sill. Perhaps there had been a shower in the night, but the air smelled unusually fresh, carrying with it the odour of damp earth and the sweet heavy scent of his roses. No sign of light so far. Good, he thought, I'm ahead of my quarry. Looking down, his garden seemed part of the night, deep in murky shadows, sunk in a dark ocean through which he could just make out the darker outline of trees and shrubs, gathered masses. Below to his left the yew trees were two columns of absolute night, and he could see the ghostly pallor of flowering trellises, bushes, coming through the dark, their colour reduced to nothing. He looked up and saw a last star, it had begun to dim, receding as the sky grew misty, opaque, though dawn was still a long way off. I must go, he thought, noticing a hint of change in the dim luminosity, if I am to catch it. He turned from the window, fumbling in his pocket for cigarettes, and opened his bedroom door. He closed it very quietly, tiptoeing along the passage past his wife's door, to avoid disturbing her.

He will be gone for hours, she thought, as she heard the floorboard creak outside her room, and then the rhythm of his footfalls down the staircase. It already seemed like hours since she had first heard him splash about in his dressing room, humming a little tune under his breath, and it would be hours before it was time to get up. No light came through the slats of the shutters, the window was a dim outline. What was the good of him tiptoeing past her room when she had heard him half an hour before through two dressing rooms? When she had told him how she could not sleep? But he forgot everything when he was in a good mood, when he thought the weather promising, both of which she had heard in the sounds which came from his room. She turned in the bed, sighing, slightly peevish and resentful, feeling the empty hours stretch ahead, how the walls and the dark space around her seemed to be closing in, till she felt she could hardly breathe and her head had begun to ache with the pressure. She put her hand to her forehead, now that the familiar throbbing had begun, the little hammer in her skull. I am an old woman, she whispered, moving her hand across her eyes, shutting them, I have begun to outlive my own children, but the soothing dark would not come: what is it about him that gives him the vigour to go off in the small hours as though time had not touched him, as though he was still a young man, no, a child, since he could be as wilful and moody as a boy? She felt as resentful now, with her head throbbing and her misery, as she had years ago, when she would lie awake worrying in this same bed, several of the children usually sick, and him absent for months on one of his painting trips. She had blamed herself for a fool then, ignoring all the warnings about quitting her class without so much as a wedding ring.

3

She stared up at the shadowy ceiling, thinking how cruel life is, so very short, but the hours unendurably tedious. Daylight was still far off, but she would not sleep now. Turning uneasily in the bed to stare at a different wall, the irony occurred to her: how had she failed to recognise those bygone years as happy? In spite of all their difficulties, worrying about money, her husband, the endless bouts of measles and feverish colds, Claude going off.

But God was punishing her now. It was back, even though she had tried to put it out of her head. She had been told in confession that it was sinful to think of Him as anything but merciful, but that was the abbé trying to be kind, she felt sure, touching her throbbing head with her fingertips and closing her eyes. She was to blame, she had sinned, and now God was punishing her with this dreadful sorrow.

She stared into the darkness punctured by the sound of a ticking clock. If only she could sleep soundly, she thought, then time would not lie on her as such a heavy burden, weighing on her as her body did, almost all of the time, she must drag it about, it had become heavy as life now, and she would be thankful to lay it down. She closed her eyes to shut out the dim surroundings, and tried to conjure up black, absolute blank, but it would not come.

Now a single bird had begun to call out in the gloom. Hidden on some branch amongst the trees round the garden its sound persisted, echoing through the cool shadowy spaces, rising upward into the dim sky. Soon it was answered by a second cry, more shrill and urgent than the first, and within a short space of time the whole garden was filled with a rising crescendo of birdsong, a frenzy of chirping sound which spilled through the entire valley, still dark, its outline scarcely visible under the sky.

In the kitchen Françoise was a little nervous. This was the first time she had been left to do the master's breakfast on her own, and she was sure to do something wrong. She tried to go over the instructions in her mind, but got in a fluster when she could not get the stove to light, even as she heard him moving about in the dining room. Doing everything calmly in the right order, that was the thing, but it would help, my girl, she muttered, if you could get up on time. Cold milk, that was simple enough, and thank God for it, since she had not yet got the knack of making coffee that cook judged drinkable, but had she said he liked his bacon crisp and his eggs a bit soft, or did they have to be cooked right through, with the whites burnt at the edges? Her fingers shook slightly as she tried to catch up on herself. She had been told that he could get in a foul mood if the food was not quite to his liking.

Françoise took her hands off the pan handle just long enough to pin back her hair, which had begun to tumble down the nape of her neck, since she had not had time to do it properly when she got up. I must look a sight, she thought. She scooped the curled rashers from the sizzling pan, but one of the eggs broke as she put it on the plate, so that the yoke ran. *Merde*, she muttered under her breath, but decided it was too late to do anything but take the breakfast in and hope he was in a good mood. Her face flushed, she picked up the tray and took it through to the dining room.

Auguste came up the verandah steps two at a time, tapped on the pane, stood for a moment, knocking his boots for possible traces of mud, and when nobody came, peered through the glass. The kitchen was empty. He knew the door was unlocked without even trying the handle, but he had never yet gone in the house without being asked to do so. Then he saw the new girl come through with an empty tray in one hand, pushing back a strand of hair with the other. She looked a bit flustered, hot and bothered, he thought, with her hair untidy and her cheeks flushed, and she was frowning as she put the tray down and turned to the stove. I don't suppose she'll last more than six months, Auguste concluded. He was just about to tap on the glass a second time when she glanced up and saw him outlined against the door. She came to open it, and for the first time noticed the day beginning outside, the dark sky lightening beyond his shoulder, and a din of birds in the trees.

He stood on the verandah and lit his first cigarette, thinking how good it was that the day was only just beginning. The house still lay in shadow, the steep slope of its roof just visible against the fading sky, rows of closed shutters lost in the dimness, with only his own window open to the indigo sky. So far he could scarcely make out the foliage of the verandah, thick with shadows as it was, but he sensed a different kind of dark in the two yew trees beyond, dense and soft, a texture that seemed to pull all darkness into itself, giving nothing back. They had grown immense over the past few years, but he had been right not to cut them down. Alice's mood was responsible, when she got over things she would not mind about the yews. After all, it was she who, years ago, had wanted him to keep the two rows of spruce down the central avenue, and if he had the place would have looked like a graveyard by now. No, there was something about those two massive shapes, the inversion of light and colour, a gravity which pinned things down. And if they took too much light from the house, how much time did he spend indoors anyhow? No, he was right, and when she cheered up a little she would see for herself how wrong she had been. If only, he thought uneasily, she would begin to rally.

He flung his cigarette on the gravel. 'Let's go,' he said, seeing the man was ready, equipment slung from both shoulders, in a hurry now, fearful that the light would change before he had got it down. He strode down the path, hearing his boots crunch on the gravel, with the gardener's footsteps following behind in an opposing rhythm. He climbed the steps of the footbridge. Below him the railway track gleamed faintly, cutting through the dark land to the far horizon, where the first thin light had just begun to spread upward, no more than a hint of light under the earth. But not enough to touch the surface of the lily pond, it still lay so deep in misty shadows that he could hardly distinguish the outline of the archipelago below. Though he heard his footfalls echo on the bridge, underneath lay a dark unexplored mystery, freshly hidden, between banks he had planned but could not now make out, stretching as far as the willow tree, its curved shape standing out against the sky. He could hear fresh water gurgling through the sluice, a sighing sound run through the long leaves of the willow. He knew, though he could hardly make out their shapes, that the lilies would be closed tight as set pearls in the dark.

He crossed the small wooden footbridge over the narrow stream that marked the bounds of his territory and was out in the open field with the dew now soaking into his trousers as he trod through the high tufted grass. He disturbed a bird which suddenly fluttered up into the dim sky, startling him, before dipping down out of sight. He had forgotten all about Auguste, trudging behind him, trying to keep up with his load, as he strode through the dim pasture, a world of shadow merging into darker shadow, more obscure shapes. The land fell away to its own secret places, shadow on shadow, fold on fold, whilst the outline of huge trees stood out against the dim sky. He heard only the swish of grasses and undergrowth as his own boots moved through, and the sound of water running in the dark under thick lines of nettle, bramble and willow. He could smell mint now, and damp earth, a cloud of insects swarmed from the reeds as he stepped into the lurching skiff and leaned forward to take the load from Auguste. Then they had pushed off and only the sound of their own movement broke the silence, oars dripping on the smooth surface of the water, the dull grind of the rowlocks, as they glided towards the spot where the studio boat with its cabin was moored.

Once aboard, whilst Auguste began to unpack the canvases, he took stock, glanced round anxiously to make sure nothing had changed. No branches had broken off in the night to change the high outline of trees rising above the riverbanks, or interrupt the smooth surface of the water. In the bluegrey hush before dawn overhanging trees met their mirror image in still grey water. He thought he had perhaps an hour.

Almost square, a total balance between water and sky. In still water all things are still. Cool colours only, blue fading to mist grey, smooth now, things smudging, trees fading into sky, melting in water. No dense strokes now, bright light playing off the surface of things, small, playful. I have broken through the envelope, the opaque surface of things. Odd that it should have taken so long to reach this point, knowing it, as I did, to be my element. I was blinded, dazzled by the rush of things moving, running tides, spray caught in sunlight. Looking at, not through. The bright skin of things, the shimmering envelope. But now, before the sunrise, no bright yellow to come between me and it, I look through the cool bluegrey surface to the thing itself.

A fish plopped in the stillness, momentarily breaking both the silence and the smooth mirror of the water. Gentle rings rippled outward and died. Auguste, leaning back in the small boat with his hand trailing in the water, wished he could have brought his fishing rod. This was boring, just sitting here. Looking down through the clear water he had seen several speckled trout swim by during the past half hour, or hour, or however long he had been sitting like this. And it was anybody's guess how much longer it was going to be. He tried to shift in the boat without making too much noise, since his body was getting quite numb. Doing nothing was difficult, and the household rule that he must not be disturbed while he was working made it more wearisome. Though Sylvain claimed he had once fallen overboard without it being noticed, until it was time to pack up, when he asked why his trousers were wringing wet. But Sylvain was a bit of a leg-puller.

Auguste could see his bulky form outlined against the dim sky, not quite so dark now, and it seemed to him that he had not moved or turned his head once in the past half hour. He found it odd, how this man worked, hour after hour, in that curious solitude, looking at nothing in particular, just this same old stretch of river where they had come to fish and swim as boys, and him diving deeper and swimming farther and more strongly than anybody, laughing, coming up with his beard dripping, and showing us how to bait a hook, like he was one of us, a man, capable of doing a man's job. Not this stuff, curious to his way of thinking, he liked something which told a story, but he had been told that folks in Paris would pay thousands of francs for one of his pictures.

He yawned, conscious of his stomach juices churning inside. The new girl was a bit stingy about food, from the looks of things, a glass of cider and a bit of burnt toast was all she laid out for him, and now he was decidedly hungry. Having nothing to do made it more obvious. He had tried, to help pass the time and take his mind off his stomach, to look around as though it was him, but it was very dull, just the same old sky without so much as a bird in it, the same old trees hanging over this uneventful bit of river, calm as anything. And besides, it was still so early that it was impossible to make anything out. The trees were just a greeny-grey blur, and the banks were lost in shadow. As for the water, there was nothing to be seen at all, not at this time of morning.

Auguste heard a sudden scraping sound as his master lit a cigarette. He saw a small bright flicker of yellow flame through the grey gloom, and for a while he could smell the smoke drifting towards him before the half-smoked cigarette was flung into the water. He had watched several float soggily downstream this morning. At the house madame had given instructions for them to be picked up from the garden paths, so she could give them to one of the beggars who came to the door almost daily, but it was hardly worth fishing them out of the water. The pleasing smell of smoke had set his stomach juices churning once more. In the old days Melanie would have put out anything cold left over from last night's dinner, but this new girl was either too stupid or too frightened to do the right thing. Still, give her time, and perhaps she would learn.

He thought of the trout he had seen slipping away through the water, how good they would have tasted, done over a wood fire with the hot flesh falling from the bone. As boys they had camped down here on the riverbank, him with Jean-Pierre and Michel, but now, well, it was awkward, he hardly spoke to them, not since they had grown up and he had started work in the garden. And then the village itself had changed, and they mostly mixed with the foreigners.

Claude laid his palette in the bottom of the boat just long enough to find a cigarette, struck a match, inhaled his first mouthful of smoke, then saw something he had not seen before and flung the cigarette from him. Something still eluded him, though now, with time running out, he thought he had almost got it. Soon dawn would come, and with it would go this hush, this cool luminosity coming through stillness. It was like sitting in the calm centre of the world, he thought, this total balance between the world and its mirror image, water and sky. He was conscious of fragility, as though he was sitting in the middle of an aquamarine bubble. That's it, he thought, as his intent eye caught a line of dark blue shadow where the river met, not sky, but its own reflected shadow.

But the light was changing now, and it was time to give up on this particular canvas. A faint streak of rose flushed the sky beyond the trees. Everything would change now, touches of pink would show in the water which would begin to shine, glinting with rose and gold, the skin of the water would become a living thing, running with fragments of the world, washing them downstream into the following night. The sky grew paler as the sun rose, light had begun to touch the trees, which broke into a thousand surfaces, leaves and branches throwing off light and colour. He could not look at his canvas now, because of what was happening on the river. Though

12

the banks were still in shadow the surface of the water in mid-stream shone like shot silk, bright pink and gold, the colour of fire between the prow of his boat and the horizon where the trees came down low and water almost touched the burning sky. Everything was always in flux, he thought, noticing a dark reddish hue close to the banks where the high trees overshadowed the water. It was both his overriding difficulty, and essential to him.

He put down his brushes, knowing it was finished for now. A sense of fatigue came over him, as he dropped tubes of colour into the box. He leaned over the side to call Auguste, and saw he had dropped off to sleep in the skiff, head propped against the gunnel, his mouth slightly open.

Two

She had lost all sense of time, as though she had been in a different place, somewhere that belonged to the night and what was left of her night thoughts, where, habitually now, she spoke to those who had only existed in the dark of her own head for years. It was odd, but during this past year of unendurable grief they seemed to have come so much closer, as though time and, with it, a long section of her own life had simply vanished, and when she hid her face in her hands to whisper to her daughter in the dark, as like as not it was her mother's voice which answered back, she was a young girl with her unhappy head in her lap, and she could almost feel the hand stroking hair which had hung down her back, or lightly touching her forehead. As though some kind of invisible wall had collapsed, and with it the visible structure of her life.

She had been squatting at the edge of the grave for so long without moving that she felt she could not move, ever again. Her knees ached, her whole body was stiff and cold. She would have to move soon, the sky above her head was growing paler, at any moment someone might pass and see her sitting like this, with her hair in disarray and the bottom of her gown wet through with dew, but that was precisely the difficulty, how could she go back, now that the wall separating night and day, the visible and the invisible, had crumbled she found it confusing, so hard to go through the motions of doing what she was expected to do, simply because she had done it for the past twenty years. Supervising the household, soothing him through his moods, smiling for visitors. For instance, they had tried to talk her out of coming to the graveyard at dawn, but what was the harm when she could not sleep anyhow? It was better to sit here, watching the dawn with her darling, hearing the first birds as she would have heard them. She felt she could breathe easier, once she was out of the house and had walked the length of the village, to this cool remote spot, so peaceful and calm in the grey hours before dawn.

But now she would have to go. I will have to leave you, my darling, she whispered, having seen how the bluegrey sky behind the high granite cross had begun to shine a clear blue, and heard the wheels of a cart grinding along the road below the church. She laid the drooping

15

roses on the earth and got up, slowly, and with difficulty. She felt, now, as though this was her home, and that the effort of pretending otherwise was becoming too much.

A cock crew, the shrill sound echoing through the clear air as a bird in another yard made a bid for the coming day. High above, the sky was a delicate blue, but its clarity was still far off. Along the winding upper road through the village, buildings stood plunged in damp cool shadow. A walled orchard with its twisted apple trees and long grass lay immersed in a pool the colour of grapeskin. The abbé, watching her stout figure walk slowly down the road, thought it was time he called, before turning back to examine a rosebush for greenfly. A woman opened her front door, shook out a cloth, and went back inside. A sparrow hopped through the dust in pursuit of breadcrumbs, but was sent off by a prowling black cat. Houses lay in the shadow of the hillside, but down towards the river a new skylight shone in the rising sun, and green meadows gleamed pollengold. By now the grey church tower at the far end of the village had also caught the sun, though nothing could touch the cold forbidding bulk of its massive structure. But it would be hours before the sun moved high enough to dry the long grass round the grave, or drink up its shadows. So far not a gleam of light had touched the tip of the new granite cross with Suzanne's name on it, though it stood so high. The tops of the oldest, highest trees had begun to catch the light now, and housefronts caught each other's sloping shadows between patches of dusty sunlight. It caught the sloping roof, chimney stack and gable, and sent probing fingers through the slats of the shutters.

For Lily, watching bars of light coming through the shutters, it was like the beginning of the world. Or was it the sound of the cock crowing before she had opened her eyes? Somebody had told her that it was the sound of the cock crowing which made the sun rise, and she had heard it long before she was fully awake. Strips of light spilled on the waxed wood floor in bright pools. In the shafts of light between window and floor she could see particles moving, dancing, and this puzzled her. Was it part of the light itself, and if so, what was it made of? Just lying in bed made her want to ask so many questions, and it was difficult to know whom to ask, because what they told her often made things more confusing.

She lay back in bed, watching the green shutters and the strips of hot dusty light coming through them, conscious of a sort of largeness all round her. First there was the room with those glowing pools of light on the waxed floor and shadows in the far corners of the ceiling and her own body so sweaty she had to kick back the sheet and blanket, then there was the huge house all round full of rooms and things so mysterious, beds and clothing with unusual scents which were part of somebody else, drawers and dressing tables cluttered with objects waiting to be found and fingered, touched and admired, bottles to be sniffed, hats and old blouses to be tried on, mirrors for looking in, a brooch to be pinned, old jars of face cream to put your finger in, and unknown picture books in the glassfronted case. Well, almost unknown. She knew just enough of this enormous rambling house with the studio and the house next door and grandmama's bureau to know how much could still be explored, and found. You could make a house under the dining table and vanish for simply ages, like Noah in his ark with the chairs pulled up close, and so far, because she was small, everybody allowed her in, cook into the kitchen, Marie into her attic room with the funny metal bed and the trunk pushed under it.

The light was creeping along, now it had touched the foot of her bed and shone in a dazzling patch of white on the sheet. She put her foot in it and felt it hot, saw the little hairs on her leg gleam the colour of honey. How long before somebody came? Time seemed to drag very slowly, to be as immense as this huge house with its multitude of unknown rooms. Tomorrow, they said, and wait till next year, but tomorrow was so far off and as for next year, it might as well be the dark side of the moon. She sat up in bed and pulled a single strand of hair in front of her face so the light shone through it, and wished that somebody would come, now that she was hungry and could hear the birds calling outside, but no sound came from within the house. And she thought that part of the fascination that her grandparents' house held for her was not just in the things to be found, furniture and pictures and the pretty blue tiles in the kitchen, but the mysterious fact of their age, the grey ash of time which clung, not just to his beard, her thick hair and the loose flesh of her features, but seemed to be exuded from the clothes they wore. In him she could smell earth and tobacco and turpentine, while her black clothes had a sweetish scent, of old perfume and talcum powder. She sniffed the skin of her arm, and it smelt of sun.

Lily wriggled in her cotton shift, and wished that nobody might come in to help her dress, that she could run round all day in something loose and cool, feeling her own skin as she did now. She wriggled some more, just for the feel of it, and tried to imagine herself escaping into the garden wearing only her nightgown, with her feet bare and the wind blowing up underneath. When she was big she would stop wearing all this stuff. She thought of the times she had struggled and even cried, been scolded for a cantankerous child for refusing to hold up her arms as another stifling layer came down over her head, or stand still as buttons and hooks were fastened. It did no good, she thought, but at least it was slightly better in the summer, as long as she did not run around and get hot.

She lifted one leg and moved her foot about in the air, then did the other one. She bounced up and down on the mattress, felt her face grow hot, and stopped to get her breath back. She heard footsteps in the passage, but they did not stop outside her door. There was a spot of light in the corner of the ceiling, trembling and quivering. In the sudden silence she could hear the steady drone of a bee near the bright closed shutters, and was overcome by the newness of everything in the world. She lay very still, to hear and watch.

* * *

As soon as she heard the birds singing, even before she opened her eyes, she knew there was something momentous about this particular day. The sound of jubilation in the chorus of birds, strong sunlight coming through the shutter slats told her it was going to be a perfect day in summer, but that was not it. Judging from her sister's footsteps moving down the passage beyond her door it was quite late, but a long night of sound sleep was also not enough to explain this sense of occasion. And then it came back to her. Pierre. Putting his hand on hers, when he was quite sure, on the bench under the lime trees. Had either of them really been sure, she thought, wide awake now, until he was holding her hand, or was it not knowing how the other one felt which made them both so nervous? She shut her eyes against the morning, wanting to relive each look and touch, hugging the memory to her, now, while it was still her own, and nobody had been told.

She got out of bed and pushed back the shutters, hooking them against the outside wall. The wood was warm under her touch, and she thought she had never seen the sky so high, blue and limpid. Turning back into the room, she poured water into the bowl and began to splash her face with it, then lifted her hair to let it run down the back of her neck. It would be best, she decided, to speak to mama, and let her intercede for them both with him. She caught sight of herself in the mirror as she was drying her face, and the pupils that stared back at her were those of a startled stranger, slightly accusing. You are too plump, they told her, and your features are

20

thoroughly ordinary. But this morning she found she could answer back, began to smile at her reflection as she lowered the towel. Ah, she thought, but Pierre wants to marry you, and found that her face was not so bad, especially when she smiled and a softer look came round her eyes.

Marthe opened the door and smiled when she saw his tousled head on the pillow, eyes screwed up tight.

'Dear, oh dear, what a sleepy head,' she said loudly, and unbolted the shutters with a clatter. It was still the same game, and she was pleased that he had not forgotten it since he went back to his father. As though this was his home, she thought, and I was his m . . . , but she would not allow herself to go on. It had occurred to her, as it had to mama, that Theodore might have begun to think of taking a second wife, now that Suzanne had been dead for more than a year, and then her sister's children would be lost to her for good. He might even decide to go back to his own country. She put her hand on his foot outlined under the cover and thought, he's grown a lot this last year, as she saw him begin to smile with his eyes shut. Then she suddenly pulled back the bedclothes. Jimmy let out a loud shriek, put his arms over his eyes, and began to kick his legs up and down in wild excitement.

'Come on, up you get,' she said coolly, practical aunt Marthe in her voice, and got up from the edge of the bed to fetch his clean sailor suit from the chest of drawers. When she turned round Jimmy was lying on the bed with his 'come and get me then' expression. This was also one of his old tricks, and it hurt her to think of him playing it with somebody else. As he surely must do, she thought, pulling him upright, knowing she had never been first with anybody. She pushed back the tousled hair and kissed him lightly on the forehead.

'You're old enough to do this yourself,' she said firmly, knowing she was inclined to pamper the boy. He pulled a face and allowed himself to go limp as a rag doll, so she could not get his arms into the sleeves. She spoke to him in the pretend cross voice she had learnt from her mother twenty years ago when she first began to help her with the little ones, only then she thought she was practising for when she had a family of her own, but it did not rouse him. Perhaps he knew she was not really angry. He was too thin, she thought anxiously, noticing the blue veins visible under his white skin, how bony his knees had become, though she tapped him firmly on the shin and said 'Keep still' so she could tie his laces.

She poured water into the bowl and passed a wet flannel over his face, not forgetting his forehead and behind his ears. The boy tilted his head back, hardly resisting as she scrubbed his face, then sat passively on the edge of the bed, humming a monotonous little tune under his breath. Legs dangling, not quite touching the floor. She picked up the brush and comb from the top of the chest, expecting a struggle if she tried to get the knots out of his fair hair, going slightly darker now. But he sat quite still. For a moment she met his eyes as he waited, head thrown back a little, and was startled by an expression she had never seen before. Was it only light from the window? A curious reflection from outside? No, it was more, not just water reflecting the sky, more like water drinking something in, some sort of deep well.

She began to comb his hair slowly, cautiously, so as not to hurt him. When the comb encountered a knot she held his head tight against her chest to minimise the strain, and he did not draw it back afterwards. She felt him lean against her as the silky strands ran freely through the comb, the weight of him against her blouse, and sat for a moment too long.

'All done,' she said brightly, and stroked his head before getting up. She scraped the fine blond hairs out of the brush with the comb, twisted them round her forefinger and threw them out of the window. An unseen current of air lifted them, she saw them drift up towards the roof in the light-filled air and out of her field of vision.

It fell across the garden, light and shadow, held by tree and shrub, reversed from light to dark in a playful pattern, a game taken up by every leaf high enough or not itself overshadowed. But the base of the trees were still heavy with dark shadow, and the verandah with its trellis of thick foliage was still cool, as Michel found when he stepped out of the studio door for a moment. Light had now caught not just the roof with its central gable, but all the upper windows not shaded by Virginia creeper, green shutters hooked back, white lace fluttering from open windows, the warm muted rose of the walls. He could hear one of the maids setting plates and cups for breakfast, the chink of spoons dropping into saucers, and stepped back into the shadowy solitude of the studio, though it was really used by the whole family now, as a sort of living room. Soon the rest of them would be down for breakfast, he could hear footsteps on the floor above, but just for a few moments he had escaped, he was all by himself with his father's pictures all round him, hung row upon row to the high ceiling, tilting slightly, as though leaning down to him. He was surrounded, he hardly needed to look at any of them, since he carried them in his mind, so much authority in a single stroke it took his breath away, but not only could he scarcely breathe from fright, he felt as though his hand and with it his will was paralysed, so that he could not move from the spot. Did he want to grow up, go away as the others had done, from this, from him? He could not decide: looking at a single brushstroke near the bottom of an unfinished canvas propped on a chair, it seemed to hold in it all magic, both power and a total authority from which he neither could nor should escape. What can I do, he thought, knowing that the rest of the family did not understand him, regarded him as odd, something of a problem, especially now that Jean-Pierre too was leaving home, to study and make a career for himself. But Jean-Pierre took him lightly, not being his son, untouched by his giant shadow and the umbilical cord of his authority. What was there to do, he thought, knowing as I do that this is all that is worth doing, but I cannot do it?

Michel heard somebody coming down the staircase and decided to go outside, to avoid being seen before breakfast.

He walked down the steps of the verandah and beyond

the yew trees, hearing birds in the branches of the limes, Marie sing a snatch of song in the kitchen and suddenly break off in a clatter of plates, the guttural cry of a man trying to control his horse in the lane, chickens clucking behind the wire. Much of the garden still lay in shadow, patches of colour caught the light as it came through dense overhanging foliage, but here and there larger patches of light made the gravel shine yellow and caught the bright stretches of flowerbeds in a glow so startling, so intense, that those in shadow seemed to have almost no colour at all. His father's blooms, he thought, knowing he could not escape from it, this perfection, it seemed to breathe for him as he heard a gentle rush of summer coming through the leaves, and yet to stifle him, deprive his lungs of their own volition. And the light was so dazzling, the colour so bright, he felt he wanted to shut his eyes to exclude the brilliant display. But he walked on down the path, looking, saw how masses gleamed in the sudden light, the dusty fragility of petals, throat and stamen exposed to the first circling wasp. Down at the end of the garden the light, having nothing to block it out, was freer, under a high thin sky of pale washed blue it shone in the milky haze of early morning, softening the pink of the rambler roses which screened off the railway track. Against the sky the willow tree quivered like a bride in a vaporous veil, while to the right of the footbridge four thin poplars stood, wraithlike, as her attendants. Light gleamed on the meadows and pastures beyond, through the same soft white mist, blurring the edges of fence and ditch, bramble, nettle and stunted willow, as the dark night's damp turned back to light and vapour. It clung to the earth's surface, hung above the valley, obscuring the source of light in a soft luminosity, which seemed to come from some dark secret within the earth, rather than the sun, though the two had perhaps colluded.

But down on the river the high banks of trees had obscured the slow passage of time, curtaining it off for sudden drama. The first hint of change had come long ago, at the point where the two banks of trees met at his centre of vision, the slow fading, followed by an intrusion of pink and gold, touching the edge of the trees with crimson. This he would have to catch. And even as he was studying the changing light it changed further, the river itself had turned to silver and gold, a moving flood, and now as the sun rose it was as though the overhanging trees could no longer hold it back, the air itself was flooded with light, white and gold, so that nothing was visible but light itself.

Three

Having sent Auguste up to the house with his equipment, he strolled round the lily pond, stopping after every few steps to look at his creation from a slightly different angle. At this time of morning the water lilies were still closed, tight round fists holding something within, but in less than an hour, when the slanting light struck that area just beyond the shadow now thrown by the largest willow tree, they would have begun to disclose their colour. He knew each moment, when it would come, by now his eye was as precise as a sundial marking, and anticipating, the hour of transmutation. But the surface of the water had to be cleaned, and now he could feel rage rising in him: what was the use of paying some lazy idiot who did not do his job? He must have a word with Felix about the other men. The pond should be like a polished mirror, but nobody quite understood just how essential this was to him. Now willow leaves floated on it, and small drowned insects pockmarked the surface.

He took a cigarette out of his jacket, struck a match, and watched the first puff of blue smoke rising as he inhaled, then forgot about it as his eyes took in, for perhaps the thousandth time, the contours of the space he had shaped. Yes, he thought, he had got it about right, the curve of the pond running inward towards the bridge with its reflected arc, two curved spans meeting, the dark mass of bamboo for emphasis, giving it just enough density, pinning it down so it would not float into the sky along with the fragile column of trees beyond. The pampas ought to be cut back a bit, and another rose trellis there, in the middle, would break the line of the bank and provide some shadow.

Having come to a decision about the rosebush, his eye studied the surface of the water, following the lily pads arranged like islands, an archipelago, seduced by the apparently random pattern until it was caught in the encircling clasp of the bridge, held there, like the belt round the curve of a woman's middle, or my hands, touching. Ah, I have you, he thought, smiling, all of you trapped, earth, water and sky. You thought you could escape, now that I am getting old, that you could run away, now I am slowing down, too old to track you down across wild landscapes. You did not think I could seduce you by luring you into my own back yard.

I have grown sly in my old age, he thought, and lit another cigarette. I used to be almost a furious madman, stalking the seasons, sun, wind and sky, to say nothing of the changing tides, coming too soon or just half an hour too late, trying to hold something which had passed on, changing into something else, dissolving. But now I have learnt to be patient, cunning. Having set an inviting trap, I lie in my hide, in wait. And it comes, the moment. Slowly, silently, it steals over the horizon and falls into my mirror.

Breakfast had been cleared away, and everybody had suddenly vanished to different parts of the house. She could hear grandmama saying something in the kitchen, but she did not know where her aunts had gone, and Jimmy had run off, knowing she could not catch up with him if he got down fast from the table without saying what he meant to do. She stepped out on to the verandah, but there was no sign of him, and it was all too huge for her to imagine she could find him, so many trees and bushes and footpaths. He might be hiding behind the greenhouse, but even if he was he would run on if he saw her coming.

Lily stood at the top of the verandah steps and began to take them one at a time, putting her right foot forward to go down, then pausing. On the third step she froze, standing stockstill with her hand on the rail as she saw a big bumble bee, hairy and with long spiky black legs, fly slowly round her head. Go away, she whispered, but did not open her lips in case it decided to fly into her mouth. Jean-Pierre, who was too young to be an uncle, had told her that bumble bees did not sting, but his telling her had not stopped it from looking thoroughly alarming. She stood rigid, only her eyes following its flight path, until it suddenly flew upward and vanished.

Three. She had counted to three. Four, she went, five, and six, landing triumphantly on the gravel with a satisfying sound of crunching as her feet hit the ground. She went back up one step to do it a second time, but almost lost her balance as she came down to land, throwing both arms out to steady herself. It was not good to fall down on gravel, once she had grazed her hand and little stones got into the wound and had to be picked out before it was washed. And when her aunt put horrid stinging stuff on it she told her about a man in the village who had cut his leg and died because nobody put any stuff on it. Both her aunt Marthe and grandmama were full of warning stories, not to do things. She was still not quite sure whether to believe the one about a plant growing inside you if you chewed grass, but now she looked rather carefully at a grass stem to make sure it was quite smooth before putting it in her mouth. She was not sure what she should be looking for, perhaps a tiny toadstool, since they were poisonous. So far each grass helm looked much like any other, but perhaps it only took something not just small, but invisible, to grow huge inside you.

A sudden gust of wind disturbed a drift of fallen rose petals at the edge of the path, and more blew down from the trellis above her head. Lily picked up a single petal, stroked its soft pink skin now brown at the edge, and tried blowing it into the air. It dropped on her pinafore, so she picked up a handful and tossed the whole lot into the air. She watched them fall slowly, flutter, catching the slanting light. Everything smelled fresh and damp now, as though the sun, where it came through the trees, was still cool and distant. She found beads of water caught in a curl of leaf, hanging from the tips of fern, cupped in a flower. But it was in a damp corner behind a heap of drying dead flowers and cut grass that she found the most astonishing sight of all, a cobweb strung between two posts, she hardly dared breathe for fear of disturbing it, a thousand drops of water gleaming in the tension of its fragile hold. The pattern perfect, each drop of water shining clear, round, holding all light within it, something that would only stay miraculous if she did not disturb, did not touch so much as one sticky thread. And she marvelled at the cunning of the spider, a creature she did not much like.

The water lilies had begun to open, layer upon layer of petals folded back to the sky, revealing a variety of colour. The shadow of the willow lost depth as the sun began to climb, light filtering through a forest of long green fingers. A small white cloud, the first to be seen on this particular morning, drifted across the sky above the lily pond and Claude, looking at the surface of the water, saw water lilies floating on cloud, the white tinged with lilac and blue, the whole partially obscured by the dark shadow from the willow tree, giving both height and depth. An effect that belonged only to still water, and one he had yet to get down.

Jimmy, perched in the bottom branch of a tree to escape marauding tigers, peered through the moving leaves and glimpsed something white, which meant they would soon reach snow level.

Far down the valley the sound of the first train of the day was coming through the stillness, a chunting and chuffing which gathered volume but not much speed, a sound so familiar in its metallic rhythm, so regular even in its irregularities, that nobody heard it, or heard it only at a subconscious level, which registers the reassuring sounds of continuity. But Lily looked up from the small stone she held in her palm and watched the white trail of steam cloud the middle distance, saw how it hung on the air, only slowly beginning to disperse long after the sound of the train had begun to fade through the distant valley. She had laid a whole row of small stones from the footpaths along the bottom step of the verandah, and now examined them one by one before putting them carefully into the pocket of her pinafore. She was struck by the infinite variety of colour, to say nothing of shape, of these tiny stones when looked at singly, since altogether on the footpaths they just looked a uniform yellow, and rather dull. And then of course it was supposed to be only dirt, when she could see that almost all the stones she had picked up were precious. She had found one dark with the colour of ruby, a small sharp one which might be an emerald, and the most precious of all, now carefully tucked into her pocket, was most likely a diamond. She took it out to admire it once more, holding it between finger and thumb against the light. It was like a solidified raindrop, clear through and through except for a rough skin of yellowish brown on one side where the edge had not been chipped away.

The leaves and branches moved, green on darker green, shadow on shadow, rising right up to the clear blue sky. A thick rustling of foliage which sighed as the cool breeze moved through it, but somehow confirmed its density, the secrecy that surrounded its branches, its lush growth. It cut out much of the morning sun, so that small lozenges of yellow light fell on the footpath, but only for a while, then light and shadow would move and disperse as the shadow branches wavering on the ground sent shadow leaves moving, and with it, the sound of air sighing in a little rush of sound, the small shapes of bright light moved also. Now it was on the toe of her shoe, hot and white, at the edge of the footpath a purple pansy fell into the random light and turned its face upward, glowing rich and dark, its markings suddenly bright. Lily always had an urge to talk to pansies, unlike other flowers they seemed to have a human face, and she thought of them as being shy, because of the way they hung their heads. And then they looked meek, somehow, keeping so close to the ground, she put her finger under the chin of one, lifted its purple head and whispered, Come on, little pansy. But its head dropped back when she let go, though it could have been smiling, because of the yellow markings, and the shape. It reminded her of how she felt when visitors came to the house and she was tidied up and shown off and made to curtsey to each person in turn. If she had a baby sister, or even a pet, she would be kind and stroke her and tell her not to be afraid of things she already knew about.

The leaves and branches moved, pale green on darker green, shadow on moving shadow, and time seemed to pass very slowly, as languidly as the breath of wind now stirring the branches. For Lily, sitting on the bottom step of the verandah, looking out and wondering where to go next, it seemed that she had already been here for ages and that the time ahead was an eternity. First there was today, and then it would be tomorrow, but beyond that things like next week were quite remote. All my life I shall be in this garden, she thought. And there will never be anything else.

An irregular shape of bright light fell on her pinafore. She put her arm across it and felt the heat, saw how the small hairs gleamed on the skin. The shadows of leaves moved across her pinafore, and she saw it in a kind of dreamy stillness, as though heat and light and leaves stirring lazily, and she now sitting in this garden were all part of a waking dream, or one from which she could never wake. And then a ray of light coming through the leaves and branches suddenly struck her face, she looked up and saw a point of light which broke outward into dazzling rays with all sorts of colours at its edges, but she could not be sure whether the prisms were in the light or in the things it touched.

Lily blinked, then closed her eyes for a moment and

felt the heat from her face turn bright crimson under her lids. But the scarlet was shot through with a nervous quiver of shifting patterns, light and dark and unidentified colour more feverish than anything she saw when she opened them again, though little black blobs now started floating over everything, rather like the small tadpoles in Jimmy's jam jar. She knew they were not tadpoles, of course, but it was odd to have them swimming about in front of everything, even the sky.

Marthe, coming out of the studio door on to the verandah, saw the child sitting by herself on the bottom step, doing nothing. I do wish, she thought, that Jimmy would not keep rushing off, but spend more time playing with his sister. The poor child must be bored, she thought, and went indoors to find something to amuse her. It troubled her that both Lily and Jimmy should spend so much time on their own, since they were motherless. She had grown up in such a big household that it seemed somehow wrong.

Four

The water lilies were fully open now, and the shadows had lost their depth. This was the light he had been waiting for, and he opened his box. The sun rose higher behind the willow tree, diminishing its reflected shadow in the water, and with it the cool expanse of bluish tones which had made the world as deep as it was high, blue and calm, with the limpid clarity of morning, and smooth as glass. The lily pond had begun to look shallow now, little more than a marshy swamp, with roots clearly visible under the water. There was more yellow in the light now, though the bluish tinge had not entirely gone from the shadowed parts of the water, dark with undergrowth, and the clear blue of reflected sky was also still visible, though only in small and broken fragments. But apart from the change in the colour of all things, he was conscious of a growing edge to things, a particularity of surfaces which made him change his technique and apply his colour impasto with a thick base of white. The full light had brought out the fleshiness of leaves and plants, their multifarious edges. The smooth surface of the water heavy with blooms and dark glossy pads.

And beyond the overgrown surface of the lily pond sunlight shimmered in the row of poplars, filtered through the green tent of the willow tree, shone on the open hillside, the sloping roofs and sheets hung out to dry in sunlit courtyards. It bounced from the glass panes of the greenhouse, settled into the dust where hens picked and strutted, drank the dark stains from the drips of wet washing and water tossed out of doors. It crept up on cool zinc milk churns, standing in shadow, and lost itself in the dark thickets of yew trees standing guard over house and garden. Indoors it fell across waxed floorboards, faded bedspreads and cushions, showing up dust in rooms where the maid had not yet been. It dried out Lily's cobweb, and turned some of the climbing roses limp on the trellis. It hummed in the wings of insects, shone on the long line of the railway track, blistered the paint of window shutters, and formed a haze, a mirage above the long grass of the pasture so that the line of trees down by the river had become dim, seemed about to dissolve in bright light, a green incandescence against the faded sky. Only between the banks of the river did it keep its purity, flowing in freedom down to the sea, a rushing silver liquid, running over sticks and stones, gleaming on the backs of quick darting fish. Elsewhere in the valley it was caught in the web of growth and dust, drying out ditches and pasture, turning to pollen in the open cups of fading, falling petals which, a few hours ago, had been full of dew. And though it shimmered with deceptive coolness in the row of poplars standing up against the pale sky, now almost white on the horizon, the cows in the meadow had all moved into the small island of shade, and the village street was empty now that the cats and dogs had slunk off to sleep in the shadow of house and wall.

Why is it I feel so tired, thought Alice, taking in the untidy litter of paper, unsettled accounts, letters which had not been answered. And although she had only just sat down she had already forgotten why she had come to sit at her bureau. It is too hot, she thought, feeling she could hardly breathe, that the bright light beyond the door had become an unbearable assault on her senses nowadays, though once she had revelled in summer weather, longing for it through the dark winter months and the cloudy uncertainty of spring.

It has something to do with change, she thought, resting her head on her hand for a moment, as she stared at the blank notepad. I am getting too slow and things change so horribly fast, light to dark, hot to cold, people coming and going, growing up or going away and dying. There, the word was out, although she had determined to put it out of her mind for the rest of the day. She put her hand in front of her eyes, knowing that the sunlight from the open door of the studio was cruel, an affront. And somebody was coming for lunch, so however tired she felt, she would have to make an effort. She fiddled with her pen, pushed back a bundle of receipts, and tried to remember the list she had intended to write. Of course it was wearing this black dress that made her feel so stiflingly hot, but she also knew she would not stop wearing it. Nothing would induce her to stop, not now. It was too soon. The world was cruel enough, changing as it did: she would keep faith.

She pushed back a strand of hair, picked up her pen, and wished she could go upstairs and lie down with the shutters closed. He hated black, never used it, that was why he had tried to persuade her to come out of mourning. But it did not seem like a year. It was stupid to feel so tired when she had done almost nothing this morning. Cider. She wrote down cider, then tried to remember what else Marguerite had said, there had been something else, but even as she stood in the kitchen she was only half listening, thinking how smoothly the household would run without her, her own cook far too busy preparing lunch to do more than shout the odd word over the clatter of pans. She dipped her pen in the ink and tried to think what the word had been. And it was true. Since Marthe had taken so much off her hands, everybody could manage quite well without her.

She looked up, at the room which had been the centre of so much everyday living, the dust and patina of years lying on everything, worn cushions, cane chairs, a patch of sunlight from the far window shining on the floor-boards, making the edge of the rug look dusty. Jean-Pierre had left a tennis racquet on the sofa, one of the girls had left some unfinished sewing in the seat of a chair. They would all go. Jean-Pierre was going, the girls would find husbands. The familiar room belied change, the shift of things, the passage of time. Suddenly it seemed to her that the room was empty, and she was no longer in it.

Germaine, who had been standing in the doorway for several minutes, watching her mother at the bureau, decided it was time to take her courage in both hands and come in. If she did not do it now it would be lunchtime, and after that it would be evening before she had a chance to speak to her, by which time her stepfather was likely to be with her, the very situation she wanted to avoid. She had come to the doorway once before, conscious of her heart thudding nervously as it had not done since the day she came to confess about breaking the water jug, and it seemed to her ridiculous that a grown woman should be so timid. How old was she when the jug shattered and made such a mess, ten, twelve? and now with her youth behind her she stood just as fearful in case he should shatter the future that she and Pierre had planned. So she had turned away, to hang round the foot of the staircase, near the kitchen door, conscious of her indecision, of the rose she had rather foolishly pinned to her blouse, while Marthe came by carrying a bowl of some sort and the new maid dashed up the stairs with a pile of unpressed linen, and she pretended to fumble for a handkerchief so that it should not look odd, her standing like this, not coming or going. So then she came back to the doorway, knowing this to be the most momentous day of her life, and that much might depend on how she went about things.

'Mama,' she said, coming into the room, and put her hand on her shoulder. She bent down and kissed her cheek, guessing that her mother's constant grief would work in her favour, if only she could convince her that Pierre really loved her, and she him. And only mama could speak to him, her stepfather, and perhaps persuade him before he made his decision.

Marthe came down the verandah steps and sat down beside Lily, who was swaying slightly from side to side with her eyes shut, smiling.

'Here,' she said. 'I've got something for you.' And set down the bowl of soapy water.

Lily opened her eyes rather slowly and gazed at her, wide-eyed, as though from an immense distance, which disturbed her. Surely the child was not going to be ill, she thought, and lightly touched her forehead: but she felt quite cool. She had spent her life looking after younger brothers and sisters, but she could not remember any of them being quite like this, remote, this curious solitude in which Lily seemed to float as easily as a dandelion clock drifting through sun and shadow. She felt it ought to be remedied in good time, and probably had to do with being motherless. Michel had something of the same mood about him, after all.

Marthe took the clay pipe and began to show her

niece how to use it, being leisurely about it. She had seen her sister loitering in the doorway to speak to mama, and she thought it would not be wise to intrude just now by going back indoors. She would make sure the children stayed outside, and did not unwittingly interrupt. Her hand shook and her voice took on a cheerful, hearty sound which she knew to be false, thinking, if Germaine marries now, I shall be the only one left behind. Which was precisely what she had always dreaded, expecting it to happen. She felt vulnerable suddenly, knowing how much her sense of self depended on the little things she constantly did for others. Fat, solid, dependable Marthe, who would vanish into thin air if nobody needed minding, or nursing. Whom nobody had ever wanted to marry, except once, and that must have been a foolish misunderstanding. She was fortunate, of course, to be able to do something, to be useful, in a home with so much comfort. She had told herself as much from the beginning, when mama left papa, and she had to get accustomed to living under the roof of a man who was not her father. So now she did what she could in the household, to help it run smoothly, conscious of looking like mama, her shadow, and frequently standing in for her. She did not mind so much now, she thought, gently pushing back a strand of dark hair from Lily's forehead, I love this child, but for a moment everything melted into a state of uneasy flux, she felt it move and shift inside her. She would not admit to jealousy, only a feeling that it was slightly selfish of Germaine to pursue her own happiness, particularly when mama was still so depressed.

* * *

The light had changed now, and the moment he had been working to seize had gone. He put down his brushes and lit a cigarette, eyes assessing the canvas. He knew he had got something now, but was too tired to think just what was still missing. Tomorrow he would wait for the right moment to come round once more. As long as nothing else changed meanwhile. And for the first time he felt hungry, his appetite roused and still stirring from the taste of smoke. The light lost its intensity, his mind its sharp focus, rambling from thoughts of lunch to visitors, new seed catalogues, ninety thousand francs owing to him, and trying to make Alice more cheerful. He sighed: sooner or later when he stopped working he always got back to the problem of trying to make her less unhappy. It had been with him during all their life together, he thought, taking varying forms at different times. Once it had been his absences, financial difficulties, her husband in the background, outbreaks of anything from typhoid to toothache, and an absurd suspicion of all the women in the world. And now Suzanne's death had become one more pretext, since the rest had gone, a focus for her underlying discontent. What was it about her, he wondered, throwing twisted tubes of colour into the box, that made her need to express so much unhelpful feeling, hostile to him, and, in the end, to life itself? Surely other women were not like this? He slammed the box shut, took down the canvas from the easel. Sometimes he felt that being religious did more harm than good, or physique might have something to do with it. But the truth is, he thought, looking up at the summer sky, she sees nothing as it is. Things are, and ought to be, simple.

Five

Lily lifted the clay pipe from the china bowl of soapy water, slowly and with care, then let the dripping overflow fall back into the dish before she brought the stem to her mouth. It seemed to her that she had been doing this for hours, with varying success, but still without the single spectacular triumph. But now, with nobody watching her, with her chest full of breath and her thoughts intent on blowing as slowly and gently as she knew how, this time she would get it right. Watching the transparent skin rise, bulge outward, begin to gleam with all the colours of a rainbow, her chest was almost bursting with wanting to gasp, stop for a second intake of breath, but she kept on, blowing slowly. She watched it grow bigger, she could see the whole world through it now, but even as it reached this maximum it began to wobble slightly, something was not quite right with its equilibrium, huge, overblown, its skin now too thin to hold it, it had begun to tip and sag from the clay rim. When she tried to let it go, little drops of soapy water splattered on to her pinafore.

Sitting on the bottom step of the verandah, Lily mused, fingering the clay pipe in her lap. She was not getting it quite right, some sort of mysterious tension between everything made it work, when it did, but how to bring it about? Perhaps she was blowing it too hard, or the soapy water was not soapy enough. Sometimes she thought it was just luck, and all she had to do was to keep trying, however long it took. She ran her forefinger round the rim of the pipe, then dipped it into the soapy water. A shadow fell across her sunlit pinafore, and she looked up. Jimmy stood with legs slightly astride, looking down at her.

'Let me have a go,' he said. 'I'll show you.' And made a grab for the clay pipe. But Lily was too quick for him.

'Go away,' she shrieked, pushing him, stamping her foot on the gravel, herself astonished at the pent-up fury that burst out of her. 'Leave me alone. I can do it.'

She could feel her face go red hot, as she put the pipe behind her back, out of his reach. As she did so her elbow nearly tipped over the bowl, but not much spilled. Her body went rigid, a resisting boulder, stiff from head to foot. Go away, she thought, not looking at him, keeping her head down so she saw only his two feet. And out loud, fiercely: 'I'm doing this.'

'Don't be a little silly,' he said, his tone cool and aloof, 'you don't think I want to play with your stupid pipe, do you? I only wanted to show you.'

'Don't want you to show me,' she muttered, still keeping her head lowered. 'I can do it for myself.' And she eyed his shoes with distrust.

There was a pause, while she waited, her body still rigid. She did not look up at him, but she could hear him breathing. What is he thinking, she thought, and waited for him to make a grab for the pipe behind her back. If he did she would struggle and it might get broken. Or somebody would come and rebuke them both, without listening first. In which case she could lose it too.

But he only kicked a bit of gravel, a token gesture, and not nearly enough to hurt. A few stones skittered round her feet, and one bounced off the edge of her pinafore. Although he had been told about not fighting girls, it was not something he took seriously. But this time she had won, had defied his authority.

'I'm going back to my secret hideout,' he announced. 'And I won't show you where it is.' His feet crunched on the gravel as he marched off, stamping slightly. Lily felt something of her triumph diminish, as though he had walked off with it, dwindling with his figure receding down the garden path, through pools of sun and shadow.

Lily sat staring at the spot, far down the garden, where Jimmy's figure had vanished. She looked at the many sunlit flowerbeds, the arched pergolas along shadowed paths, and the high trees stirring above her head, and the world seemed suddenly empty. It was nearly always like this, if she wanted something and got it by fighting: somebody would punish her for it. Lily blinked off the tears in which garden and sky had begun to swim, and turned her attention to the white clay pipe.

She dipped the head in the bowl, took a deep breath, and started to blow down the stem. Slowly the luminous curve rose, strong and sure as her own breath, she saw its edge shining and felt how her breathing continued steady, all her attention was focussed on it now, controlling the even gentle flow without jerks or sudden gasps, and this time, as the bubble continued to grow, round and clear, shining with the reflected glory of the world, she knew it would be all right. It sat strong, with an inner tension to keep it so, on the rim of the cup, round, iridescent, and perfect. Slowly, moving with great care, Lily took the stem of the pipe from her mouth and gazed at the shining globe. Then, with a flick of her wrist she sent it into the air, to float upward, a clear sphere holding all the light and colour of the world in its transparency. The few seconds during which it held were enough for Lily. Memory holds the shining bubble, bright with the newborn glory of the world.

Six

'That was a beauty,' said Marthe, coming down the verandah steps. From the expression on her stepfather's face as he stood on the path below she was afraid the child sitting down there might be annoying him. He had that distant brooding look which spelt trouble, a dark cloud gathering round him before the storm, so there was only one thing to do, stay out of sight.

But he did not hear her. Coming up the garden path, he saw the small figure caught in light, the white pinafore shining, and for a moment he had lost all sense of time, it was one of his own children sitting on the step, he looked down the green tunnel of memory and saw Mimi trying to walk towards him, the shadow of foliage falling between them. He had a wheelbarrow, and it stood in the sun, in the blazing hot sun with the gravel shining yellow as the sunflowers high above his head, and summer had come round in spite of Camille's death, and her child was walking. But this garden was not the same garden, though the child sat in a tunnel of greenery which was all her own in spite of death, though his mind held the other place, high with sunflowers, and Mimi barely walking. This place was darker, had more shadow, partly because of the yew trees, but the child he saw, somehow remote in time, and surrounded by shadows, moved in a circle of light which he could not touch.

I am no philosopher, he thought, fumbling for a cigarette, but if continuity is anything, it is in this. Bright pictures in the dark of the mind, each an echo of something, but still unique.

'Come along, child,' Marthe added, in her most officious bustling tone. 'I think you need cleaning up for lunch.' And she turned over Lily's palms, still conscious of her stepfather standing just a few yards off, his dark eyes watching them both. It made her nervous, so she tried too hard to be playful, giving the small hand a brisk little pat, allowing the child to chatter on without hearing a word, while she thought, perhaps somebody had damaged one of his precious plants, in which case there would be hell to pay, she had warned Jimmy about not climbing so much, but he was only a child. She picked up the bowl and tipped the dregs on to the gravel, thinking if his work has gone badly this morning, then nobody will be able to do anything to humour him, and lunch will be quite spoilt. She got up, pulled Lily to her feet, and told her to go indoors.

'Ask Marie to give you a wash and tidy while I find Jimmy.' She was conscious how much she looked like her mother now, stout, middle-aged. She even heard an echo of her voice as she spoke the words. It had started years ago, mimicking mama's authority to try and get obedience from the younger ones, the two boys especially, but now it had become part of her. She was conscious of it now in regard to her stepfather, his continuing approval. It was his household, and even mama respected it.

Lily was skipping from one leg to the other, then back again. 'I want to find Jimmy,' she said, and took Marthe by the hand.

Françoise had come out on the verandah to arrange chairs round the table and sweep off the fallen leaves and petals. The dull sound of wood scraping on wood, then a cloth being shaken out.

Claude put his thick square fingers on the child's head, as though feeling the curved skull, and Lily had to stop jumping up and down. As usual, her wondering eyes were caught and held by the huge spread of his grizzled, bushy beard.

'I don't want her left alone too much, and you're the one who can do most.'

Marthe flushed, and tightened her grip on the child's hand.

'She has always relied on you,' he added, intending it

both as a compliment and a statement of fact.

But Marthe was thinking: not once had he asked Michel or Jean-Pierre to stay at home and keep her company, they could go off for hours without him saying a word. Something to do with daughters, in his mind.

'I think Germaine is with her,' she murmured, and immediately wondered if she had said too much. Behind her she could hear Françoise and Marie laying cutlery for lunch. Moving leaf shadows on the footpath between them, on his jacket. Both of them screened off by foliage from the full heat of the day, but she felt sweat trickling down the side of her neck.

'I'd better find Jimmy,' she said, 'and get him cleaned up in time for lunch.'

The sun was high now. Down by the lily pond Gaston finished clearing the muddy tangle of undergrowth by the bridge and thought, judging by the sun, that it would soon be time to break for a bite to eat. His rumbling stomach would have told him so even if the sun had not stood high overhead, directly above the lily pond, shrinking what little shadow remained, fading colours, the pink rambler roses on the fence by the railway track looked almost white, and the grass had turned a tired yellow. The row of poplars on the skyline beyond the bridge seemed little more than a mirage, a shimmer of silver and grey. He was thirsty as well as hungry, and his back ached from so much stooping. That was the worst of this job, he thought, what it did to your back. Not like ploughing. He wiped the sweat off his forehead with the back of his hand. Jimmy, watching him from above, had changed his identity several times, but now concluded that he was definitely an unfriendly Indian, in which case he should take him by surprise and jump on him from above, gripping him by the shoulders and holding a knife to his throat. Gaston was a good sport, but he was not sure he could do it from this branch, and besides, he did not have a knife. Perhaps he is only a Sioux, he whispered, and then could not remember if the Sioux were friendly or not. He would have to ask father, when he got back. Sioux, what a curious word it was. Like Ohio. Father came from Ohio, and had taught him how to pronounce it. America was full of funny words and one day, when he was grown up, he would go there.

Jimmy swung his left leg over the wooden handrail and hung there, both feet dangling, hands holding on. He thought the man below him might be setting a trap for an otter, or catching fish in some odd way, by tickling, probably. He considered trying to communicate with the man by sign language, but maybe Gaston would laugh. He was beginning to feel hungry, having travelled on horseback for days, through primeval forest and grassy plains. Perhaps he should shoot a buffalo: could one eat buffalo? He was not sure, but he thought deer unlikely. The problems of decision had begun to multiply as the days of his journey stretched ahead of him, and he was getting a bit tired. He leaned against the length of the steep curving rail, his cheek against the wood. He could see little sparks of sunlight coming through the foliage when he looked up, flashing white as the leaves moved, but he could see colours in it too, coming and going too quickly. Gaston had straightened up and was putting his tools on the wheelbarrow. Should he ask for a ride on his back now that he had finished clearing the pond? But that would mean giving himself away, and besides, he was feeling drowsy now, with the heat. Gaston had rough brown hands and would gallop really fast if nobody was within earshot. He began to push the wheelbarrow down the path, stomping on the gravel in gumboots. The sound faded, solitude swept back like a huge wave, he could feel it, high as the trees, higher, the world was immense, a sudden gust of wind through the trees made all his limbs tingle as he held on tight.

Seven

The doorbell rang as Alice was inspecting the table on the verandah, shifting place settings slightly, smoothing down the cloth. She pushed a wine glass a little to the left and saw Marthe saunter up the middle path as though she had all the time in the world, leading a child by each hand. She was playing some sort of game with them, swinging their arms as she held them, one by each hand, and they all laughed and shouted a word she could not hear as their arms suddenly swung up into the air to some kind of rhyme, she supposed. Marthe is getting much too stout, she thought, not that it matters now. And she saw that the new girl had forgotten about her husband's black pepper, turned to go to the kitchen, when she heard an unfamiliar voice in the studio. She smoothed down her black dress, nervously touched her hair to make sure it was secure, no wisps coming down, when Octave stepped out on to the verandah, smiled, and bowed over her hand. He was dapper as always, dressed impeccably in English tweeds, in spite of the summer weather. Master of the exaggerated gesture, the sardonic smile, his brown eyes nevertheless looked kindly at her, as though he was conscious of her fragile state, the ruin of this past year.

'You look well,' she said, knowing that he had been in poor health. And it was true, she thought, he had aged very little, in spite of it, to say nothing of his difficulties with that wife of his. She found she liked him more now that he had begun to come without her, and she even pitied him a little. Claude might think her handsome, but she had not turned out a good wife to him. Of course he could be difficult, she knew that, but artistic husbands were bound to be moody and unreasonable at times, as she had reason enough to know. She smiled at him, having caught sight of Claude in the garden below, and Octave returned the smile as part of the general greeting. Besides, she thought, he had been more than a good friend, a staunch ally, and her loyalty must be to him.

Marthe came up the verandah steps, hot and flustered, holding an untidy, unwashed child by each hand. She did not seem to mind how she looked, wiped her hand on her skirt before giving it to Mirbeau, and laughed.

Then, mercifully, she took the children indoors to be tidied up. Alice wished she minded more what impression she made, but Octave had turned from the door and was looking down at the garden with the keen eye of the expert. Apart from her husband's work, nothing interested him more.

'You've beaten me this year, I think.'

Octave stood at the top of the verandah steps, lit a cigar, and gave a sigh of pure pleasure.

'It's coming on,' said Claude modestly.

Françoise appeared in the doorway, waiting rather shyly to catch madame's eye. Instead she caught the quizzical stare of the guest as he turned, and blushed furiously. She had heard rumours about him, the wicked things he wrote.

'Shall I sound the gong for lunch, madame?'

Alice could not think where the boys had got to, but she supposed they could not wait much longer.

'Yes please. But ask Marguerite not to serve up at once. I think we can give them a few minutes more.'

The girl withdrew, after a wary glance in the direction of the visitor.

'Oh, and Françoise, the black pepper,' she called through the studio door.

'The trouble with servants,' said Octave airily, 'is their tendency to get corrupted by the people they serve.'

'She's new,' Alice murmured absently, touching cutlery, trying to think if anything was missing from the table. Claude never rose to bait of this kind, though he liked to hear his old friend sounding off on one of his attacks on the world.

'It's the theme of my new book,' Octave went on. 'I've brought you an advance copy.'

The gong booming through the house almost drowned his last words. Claude had pushed out a cane chair for his friend, and was now pouring the first glasses of wine.

'As I see it, the servant system is one of the greatest impediments to social progress.' Octave took a sip of wine, raised his eyebrows appreciatively, and continued: 'It is not just that they are exploited. The worst of it is that servants, working in the houses of the rich, of the bourgeoisie, acquire their failings. They become greedy, acquire a taste for luxury, they even, heaven help us, become snobs, and begin to despise their own kind.'

Claude looked mildly amused, a glass of wine in his hand, his eye on a half open rose in the trelliswork near his friend's left shoulder, but his wife's expression had turned to a puzzled frown.

'I don't know how we could manage,' she said, thinking how both of them liked good food. 'I've brought six children into the world. Besides, people need jobs.'

'Ah,' said Octave, before taking another sip of wine. 'But what about *their* children, who looks after them? Well,' he added, smiling wickedly, 'I suppose it is highly irresponsible for the lower orders to indulge in parenthood.'

Germaine had come through the studio door, something self-conscious about her manner as she tried to slip unobtrusively into a chair.

'Poverty with a young family,' said Claude gruffly, 'always brings misery, particularly for the woman. Class has nothing to do with it.'

He spoke with a depth of feeling which sobered his guest and brought a moment of silence round the table. Although his first wife was never mentioned, they had all known her, just as they understood the reason for the heavy silence that surrounded Camille's name: he felt partly responsible for her suffering. Only Germaine, thinking of Pierre, assumed he had already considered the proposed marriage and dismissed it. She felt tears pricking, and glanced pleadingly at her mother for a sign of support, or comfort. But Alice was engrossed in her own memories, not just of Camille, but of her first husband's financial ruin, and the ensuing chaos. Giving birth to Jean-Pierre in a railway compartment, for instance. The memory made her flush even now.

From below the verandah came the sound of laughter, words tossed to and fro. Up the steps, taking them two at a stride, came Jean-Pierre, a more subdued Michel behind him.

'Van Buren has bought an automobile,' said Jean-Pierre, laughing. 'And it's bright yellow.'

His thin face was animated above the dark beard which now concealed his mouth and chin, something his mother still had not got used to. She watched him, trying to match his features to those of the boy she had known, the child she had touched so often. Behind him lurked Michel, quiet and sullen: what had got into him lately? He sat down without a word, looking at nobody. Had she failed him somehow? Alice could not remember a time when she had not treated him just like her own children.

'So,' said Octave, 'the peace of our lovely countryside

is to be further disrupted.' The sound of an approaching train coming down the valley grew louder. He paused, more for effect than because he could not be heard, raising a sardonic eyebrow as it rattled past the bottom of the garden, chuffing out a cloud of steam. 'As I was saying, the peace of our lovely countryside—' and waited for the laughter to subside.

'Van Buren, you said. Trust these foreigners to get in first. Suppose the fellow isn't a Jew by any chance, eh?'

He fiddled with his moustache, put on an affected voice and grinned, knowing his audience. It was part of a continuing act whenever he visited, and Jean-Pierre, hanging on his every word, was already quite breathless.

Marthe had come out of the house, bringing the two children, and there was a general shuffling of chairs as everyone settled round the table and a second cushion was found for Lily. Octave put down his glass to allow his host to refill it.

'But I must confess I'm annoyed with this foreign fellow for beating me to it. I was going to surprise you the next time I came down. Though I can't promise,' he added, glancing at Jean-Pierre with mock gravity, 'that it will be yellow. It would be a little young for a man of my years and reputation.'

Jean-Pierre giggled. Alice had pushed back her chair as Marie came along the verandah with a large dish of marinaded mushrooms.

'I thought it should be red myself. But my lady wife was against it.'

Hearing the general laughter, Lily joined in, with no idea of its cause, just to be part of it. Her high voice sounded in a thin piping descant above the rest. Jimmy glared scornfully at her, and pulled a grimace. Lily stuck out her tongue.

The large shallow dish passed rather awkwardly from hand to hand. Marthe gave a small portion to Lily, and allowed Jimmy to help himself whilst his aunt Germaine held the dish for him. But now Claude was sticking his fork into a mushroom. It was the testing time, as the whole family knew. Alice, looking anxiously to the far end of the table, saw him savour the first mouthful, slowly testing it on his tongue with a brooding expression, almost as though he was listening to an inner voice.

'Not bad,' he said, and began to tuck in with relish. All round the table an invisible tension eased off, and Alice breathed out.

'Delicious,' remarked Octave, dabbing his moustache with a napkin, and thought he had done his duty to the lady of the house.

Alice smiled. 'The cook we have now is such a treasure. Not like the old days.'

Marthe got up to settle Lily, who was slipping off her two cushions and looked in danger of vanishing under the table.

'Why don't we get a car?' Jean-Pierre spoke very loudly, conscious of his own youth and daring. His first glass of wine and the presence of Octave sitting opposite had made him bold. Marthe and Germaine glanced at each other, then at their stepfather, who shook his head without looking up and muttered something about 'new-fangled objects.'

'We should move with the times,' argued Jean-Pierre. The fact that he was leaving home and had begun new studies made him feel tremendously ahead of things, part of the new century.

Claude snorted as he jabbed his fork into the mushrooms. 'Is that what you call it?'

Michel was watching with his sleepy eyes, but said nothing. Alice, who had been fussing over the fact that the maids had forgotten to put bread on the table, had hardly heard a word. Now she got up and walked the length of the verandah to tap on the kitchen door.

Jean-Pierre lowered his voice: 'It might help to cheer up mama. You know how she loves speed.'

'That's true.' Germaine glanced at her brother, then ventured to add: 'I think Jean-Pierre is right. It would do her good.' It was so rare for her to argue against her stepfather that she felt herself flushing, and her words faltered slightly.

'Well, I'll think about it,' Claude muttered grudgingly, knowing that, since it was not the first time the topic had come up, it was unlikely to be the last. He was finding the notion increasingly hard to resist. Not for himself, but something had to be done about Alice, he thought, watching his wife as she brought the bread basket to the table. Get her out of the house, that was the thing. If a trip abroad this winter did not do the trick, then perhaps he should consider buying an automobile.'

'They're hideous things,' he said. 'Noisy and smelly.'

'What is?' asked Alice, vaguely trying to catch up on

61

the conversation as she passed the bread basket down the table. Her black dress looked faded as it caught the light.

'So is a horse,' said Jean-Pierre quickly, mighty pleased at his own wit. He was a man now, he thought, a man among men, and he grinned at the witty, notorious Octave with a look of daring complicity. Now that the wine had begun to go to his head the light and leaves in the garden were becoming curiously indistinct, in the background things moved in a continuous dazzling blur, and his awe and fear of the man at the top of the table had diminished to a small point at the back of his head which somehow gave meaning to his daring. He looked down the table to his sisters, wanting to catch their approval, but Marthe was fussing like an old matron over the two children and Germaine looked very odd, as though she had not heard a word, a sort of absent expression on her face, and a little smile which he knew had nothing to do with him. Which left only Michel, his old playmate, silent and sulky as usual, taking no part in the conversation, but listening, watching, from under those heavy white eyelids, as though sitting in judgement on everything and everybody.

'Come on, back me up, Michel.'

Everybody looked at Michel, because they had forgotten about him, and became anxious once reminded. Michel shifted uneasily in the cane chair, making it creak when he ought to have spoken. Marie and François had come out to clear the table of the plates and dishes from the first course, a noisy distraction which eased the tension enough for Michel to say, in a low voice which, perhaps, he hoped would not be heard:

'He doesn't approve of progress.'

It was something he had done since childhood, but even now Michel did not refer to his father directly. A kind of nebulous third person, too big to be named or looked at directly, as though some awesome higher power were involved, something which could not be involved safely.

Octave slapped the flat of his hand on the table and leaned forward.

'But there you are wrong, my friend. The automobile presents an enormous stride forward—think of the freedom it gives you! No more sticking to railway timetables. The whole of France, the whole of Europe is yours, at a whim. Inventions like the automobile and the telephone will put an end to our militarist politicians and make the twentieth century the age of peace and the common man. How can they make us go to war against a man when we have toured his country in our automobiles, and he ours? How can you kill a man when you can speak to him on the telephone?'

'Suppose he doesn't speak French?' asked Jean-Pierre, still in a state of high elation.

'German is a hideous lingo,' muttered Claude, and recalled a pension in Italy where the very sound had driven him mad with irritation.

'Let me tell you,' and for once Octave was wholly serious, wagging an admonitory finger, 'that the Germans are industrially and technically far more advanced than we are. Their language may be hideous but their roads are far better than ours, and no doubt their automobiles are too.'

'So, what's to stop them marching in again using automobiles this time?' asked Claude, as Françoise came through from the kitchen with a pile of fresh plates.

'Our roads are so terrible that they'd soon get stuck,' said Octave. A burst of loud laughter startled Marie, who was just bringing the hot, heavy main dish, but she managed to set it down before madame without mishap. 'No, but seriously,' Octave continued when the laughter had subsided, 'in the long run these new inventions are for everybody, ordinary men and women. And, given the means of communicating with each other, without being hoodwinked by their villainous betters, ordinary men will not fight each other.'

'I hope you are right,' said Alice with a sigh, and lifted the lid of the main dish. A delicious smell rose in the cloud of steam, and the focus of attention shifted to Alice's end of the table, as she stood to serve more easily. Marie and Françoise were placing side dishes at the far end of the table, where they could find space.

'Coq au vin,' announced Jean-Pierre, having recognised the smell even before his mother had dished out the first spoonful. He suddenly felt ravenously hungry.

'I hope she's got the seasoning right this time,' Claude watched the first plate being passed down the table to his guest.

'Of course she has,' Alice remarked calmly, giving the serving spoon a firm tap on the base of the plate she was holding before handing it on. She turned to their guest.

64

'He forgets that not everyone likes pepper as much as he does.'

Claude grunted, a bottle of wine between his knees as he tugged at the corkscrew. Marthe had lifted the lids of the vegetable dishes and waited for Octave to serve himself. She fished out a rose petal which had dropped amongst the small round potatoes, and gave two to each of the children. Lily's napkin had slipped out from under her chin and she tucked it in more firmly. At the far end of the table Octave was telling some scandalous story involving several politicians and bureaucrats in a hilarious farce of bungling stupidity, but she had missed a vital link in the story when she tried to stop Jimmy reaching out across the table, almost upsetting his grandmother's glass of wine. Germaine, who should have been keeping an eye on him, looked flushed and absentminded, fiddling with her fork and scarcely touching the food in front of her. Jean-Pierre's high-pitched laugh marked the climax of the anecdote. Marthe, having heard only snatches, wondered if it was true, and if so, how he knew about it. Or whether it was meant to be listened to as one of his moral fables, and understood as such. Looking at his smooth head over the clutter of dishes and long-stemmed glasses, it occurred to her that he might not know the answer himself. He would raise his eyebrows in that odd fashion and say something mocking if she dared to ask, but of course she would not.

'Telephone poles are ruining my landscapes,' grumbled Claude, picking up on a newly installed telephone which had been referred to in the story.

'Now that is serious,' said Octave, pulling a chicken

bone out from between his teeth.

Claude described how he had gone back to a favourite haunt a few weeks ago and found it marred beyond recognition. The family, who had heard it before, sat politely while the story ran its course, knowing that this was the kind of thing visitors would listen for, and carry off respectfully. But Octave was an old hand, an expert, and argued for new ways of seeing. Sensing an edge, perhaps even a touch of danger, they began to listen properly, with fresh interest. Octave won the discussion by bringing in the Gare St Lazare, as an undoubted product of the machine age, which his friend had chosen to paint in the past.

'You're right.' Claude passed his plate down the table, catching Alice's eye, and she took the lid off the casserole to serve him a second helping. 'And wrong,' he added, waiting for the plate to come back to him. As a man of few words, he felt bound to add: 'I just feel it, that's all. My instinct.'

Germaine had been half listening to the conversation, half not. Now she passed the plate on to her stepfather and sat back, thinking that the man beside her would appreciate her Pierre, with his ideas about inventing machines for the future. She was not hungry, but she could not lean too far back without getting snared in thorns from the climbing roses. It was still hot, but a passing breath of wind through the high trees and dense foliage at her back sent a sensuous shuddering sensation right through her.

'What is the good of travelling if there's nowhere left to go?'

The words seemed to come to her from a great distance, and somehow they had nothing to do with her. It was as though all the problems in the world, the things people often discussed, if only for something to do, could not concern her, not now, and she was cocooned in a marvellous glow of tingling sensation, a soft feeling which would keep her safe for ever. And this odd immunity, this was the gulf between yesterday and today. Between all my yesterdays, she thought, gazing into the liquid light of the water jug, and tomorrow.

'Mademoiselle Germaine is looking particularly fetching today.' Octave had leaned forward, elbow propped on the tablecloth, to pass his plate down, and noticed something about her complexion, the little rose pinned to the neck of her blouse, a soft shadow in her glance which had not been there before. Startled and embarrassed to find herself suddenly the focus of attention, a hot flush turned her face crimson. She smiled as she took his plate, but avoided meeting his eye.

Françoise had come from the kitchen with the salad. She hovered in the background, uncertain what to do with the dish, since the table seemed so full. Perhaps she had brought it out too soon? She was about to go back with it when madame said 'No, no', and got up to clear a space. Two of the vegetable dishes were empty, and removed.

Alice saw her husband look into the tumble of green leaves with a critical frown, and said: 'My dear, Marguerite is quite capable of dressing a salad. But there is a pepper mill by your plate.' She felt it was unfair to submit a guest to his habit of dressing a salad at table

67

and wildly over-seasoning it.

Jimmy, unable to eat much more and bored by the words and laughter passing to and fro round his head, had been swinging his legs under the table. Now he took a crust of bread and fitted the curve between his teeth and his upper lip, making it stick there. He grinned widely at Lily, who was watching him across the table. Lily looked solemn, then tried to reach the bread basket, could not quite touch it, and knocked over the wine glass. Immediate cries, the stain spread through the cloth, grandmama had got up and was placing a napkin under the wet spot, then scattered salt on top. Jimmy grinned more broadly, and the crust slipped out of his mouth. Lily, feeling the tears prick, saw him push it back, then wrinkle his nose and cross his eyes. If the clock strikes now, thought Lily.

'So the philistines have accepted him at last,' Octave was saying. 'After all that fuss over the Balzac figure.'

'Not that you'd think so, to judge from the main exhibition,' growled Claude, tossing the salad.

'Liberty, vulgarity, stupidity—what do you expect, my friend?' remarked Octave, banging his fist on the table. His glass tinkled against the water jug.

Lily glanced at her aunt, whose head was turned away, and made another attempt to reach the bread basket. Her fingers just touched the edge. She tugged at the table-cloth, trying to shift forward in her seat. Across the table, Jimmy was watching her, sitting quite still, with a sly look in his eyes. But now one of the cushions began to slip from under her.

'Keep still, child,' said Marthe, turning round just in

time to adjust the cushion under her. 'Or I'll take you up now, before the sweet.'

But grandmama leaned forward and put her white plump hand on her arm, so she could smell the funny odour that always seemed to come from her.

'Is there something you want, child?' she asked kindly, but Lily just shook her head, pressing her lips together. It always seemed to come out of her clothes, thought Lily, sitting rigid, watching the brown flecks on the back of her grandmother's hand, and half the smell was sweet, like flowers, like the bottle which stood on her dressing table, but under it was something not so nice, something sharp and acrid, a mixture of skin and powder and sweat, and through it all something even more powerful, the pungent odour of mothballs. Her clothes smelt of years of folding, putting away, as though the fresh air could not get at them, however much she walked about.

Everything is different about old people, she thought, their shape under the clothes they wear, their colour, everything. Those little brown flecks on the skin, for instance, and something flaccid, soft and loose about grandmama's cheek when she was expected to kiss her. Soft and dry, not unpleasant: just different. But grandpapa, who also had brown flecks on the back of his hands, his skin was anything but soft, firm and bristling with beard, and from his clothes came an odour of tobacco, which she liked. Strong earthy smells which came from out of doors, and sometimes tiny particles of colour caught round his fingernails, which she thought fun. As though he had come away with bits of river, field or sky clinging to him, after making such things. Like she and Jimmy after using plasticine. Everything about grandpapa, she thought, staring at his bearded head on the far side of the water jug, everything about grandpapa was on the surface, outside where you could see and hear and touch it, but grandmama was just the opposite: the secret of grandmama was concealed in her black dress, in the folds of her gown and what she might wear underneath. It was buried in her face, too, in the slack mouth and soft white cheeks, and the pale eyes that said nothing. Only now and then one got a whiff of it, her secret, in the faint odour coming from her clothes.

A kind of drowsiness seemed to settle over the table and those sitting round it, a momentary pause, as though each person had retreated into some space behind the eyes. Insects hummed in the rambler roses, and the drone seemed to grow louder, more persistent, in the lull. Marthe saw a leaf shadow stir across the guarded contours of Michel's face. A thousand insects hummed in the thick foliage, and the wine had made her feel quite sleepy. She saw young Jimmy yawn and lean for a moment against her sister's shoulder. Germaine looked flushed, and small beads of moisture stood on her upper lip. A strand of loose hair was hanging down the side of her collar. High above the verandah the sound of birds chirping in the treetops, and Octave was using a toothpick with studied concentration.

The servants had cleared the main dishes and plates, leaving the tablecloth slightly wrinkled, with bread-crumbs and salt scattered on it. The damp patch had dried and Alice removed her napkin, then smoothed the cloth, but only in a desultory fashion. Lily was staring at the light dancing in the water jug, trying to think how it had got into the clear shimmering liquid, what made it move and tremble so. She felt as though she was being hypnotised by this small area with its quivering slip of liquid silver, so that everything else in the world receded into a dim fog, and almost vanished.

Françoise set a bowl of strawberries on the table, but still nobody moved. Octave sucked on his teeth, looking thoughtfully at nothing in particular, then smoothed the ends of his moustache. A wasp had begun to circle round the bowl, at first wildly angular, then gradually honing in on the ripe glistening fruit. Alice put out a hand to shoo it off as it settled, but only disturbed it for a moment. By now it had been joined by a second wasp, and Jean-Pierre got up and began flicking at them with his napkin, making a lot of wind and knocking over an empty glass as he did so.

'They won't harm you if you leave them alone,' he announced, but continued to flick with his napkin. Marthe saw Michel giggle quite unexpectedly, quietly to himself, then look round to make sure nobody had noticed his nervous mirth. He glanced first at his father, then round the table, but by this time Marthe had turned to Lily, who was flinching from the flight of a wasp.

'It's all right,' she said, as Lily leaned against her, making a whimpering sound in her throat.

Françoise had come back with a stack of dessert plates, and Marie followed behind with a dish of whipped cream in one hand and a bottle of liqueur in the other.

'You must see my new specimens in the orchid house,' said Claude.

Octave split his toothpick in half and put it down. 'I knew there must be something,' he said. He had intended the remark to sound slightly envious, but instead it came out more truthfully, fond and full of quiet contentment.

Urged by his hostess, Octave helped himself to a few strawberries, then took the bottle of liqueur from Jean-Pierre. 'I've got a lot of greenfly this year,' he remarked, and sighed heavily, as though he was thinking of more profound problems that waited for him at home.

Alice glanced at him with concern, then looked meaningfully at her husband, trying to catch his eye, meaning to say 'I told you so'. But it was as if he had not heard. Claude had lit a cigarette and seemed to be thinking of something else, his eyes had that far off look she had seen so many times during their years together. A drift of blue smoke now hung on the air, its odour mingling with the faint smell of roses and food. At least it will send off the wasps, she thought, trying to console herself for the sudden pang she felt, the twist and flutter inside her.

She could hardly explain it to herself, she thought, helping Jimmy to split a large strawberry, too large to eat in one mouthful. It was ridiculous, considering his age now, and their position. But something in him still escaped her, in spite of everything she had done. And though he should by now have shared her opinion of Alice Mirbeau, her meaningful look had gone unanswered. And to make things worse Belle-Isle had suddenly sprung into the conversation, Octave was telling Jean-Pierre how the three of them had been stranded offshore by rough seas, such fun it had been, though not for her, left behind with a brood of constantly ailing children, and tedious everyday household duties.

'My Alice togged out in men's clothes,' Octave reminisced fondly, as though speaking of a different woman. 'She took over the landlord's kitchen to make sure we ate well. What year was that—eighty-six?'

'Eighty-seven, I think.' Claude had the same indulgent, rather absent smile. 'She looked very fetching, I remember, in a fisherman's cap.'

Jean-Pierre and Michel were both listening intently, and the two girls were almost as interested. Alice got up abruptly, dropping her napkin, and went indoors. Marthe and Germaine glanced at each other, slightly uneasy. Marthe shrugged helplessly, answering her sister's raised eyebrows, and both leaned forward to hear the rest of the story.

'Though I had a suspicion,' remarked Octave slyly, 'only a suspicion, mind—you were very polite—that you were dying to get rid of us, to get back to work.'

'Well,' his friend looked only mildly embarrassed. 'You were very understanding. Didn't you go mushrooming, or something?'

Alice suddenly stepped out through the studio door, picked up her napkin, and sat down. 'Coffee's coming,' she muttered, frowning, not looking at anybody.

Lily was pushing a last strawberry round and round her plate. Her will to get it on to her spoon had been sapped, by heat, fatigue, and too much food.

73

'Come on,' said Marthe, noticing the glazed look in Jimmy's eyes, the dark dilated pupils, and Lily with her left elbow on the table, propping her heavy head. 'I think it's time I took you up for your afternoon nap.'

Jimmy slipped down from his seat, then reached for a last vanilla biscuit. Marthe had already gone indoors, her hand on his sister's shoulder. He followed them, and as he stepped over the threshold, into the sudden shadow, he felt he had momentarily lost control of his body, as though he was stepping into a void, falling forward, blotches of colour floating across the high dark spaces, after-images of the bright glowing garden outside disturbing his vision.

A blackbird had hopped up the verandah steps. Germaine watched it pause, listen, the small head cocked to one side, alert for a sudden sound or motion. Bored with the conversation, she wished the lunch would finish and the guest take his leave, so that her future could be decided, now, soon. She took the bread which Jimmy had left on the tablecloth and threw some crumbs to the bird, moving her arm slowly to avoid startling him.

Her stepfather was pouring eau-de-vie. 'Home grown.' He lifted his glass to the light. 'Made from our own fruit.'

Octave took a sip, allowing the liquid to linger in his mouth. 'To all our yesterdays,' he said, raising his glass, 'this . . .' he wriggled his thick moustache, 'distillation of light, come to fruition.' He looked pleased with himself, as though he had just delivered a journalistic flourish in print. Jean-Pierre wondered if he was drunk, but that was

74

part of his charm, never quite knowing how serious he was being.

The bird had fluttered up into the branches, leaving a few crumbs on the wooden steps. How he does go on, thought Germaine, looking at the empty spot where the bird had been. Thinking of the years she had heard him hold forth, showing off. Something men did. From the kitchen at the far end of the verandah came the sound of washing up, plates clattering, one of the girls had begun to sing above the noise, and suddenly a second voice joined in at a lower pitch. It surprised her now, to hear it, and for a fleeting second she wondered what it might be like to be such a girl, born to work from dawn to dusk, instead of this. Meaning this endless continuum of days, sitting in on other people's conversation, being polite at table, not hers, sitting about to receive visitors who had no interest in her anyhow. And yet there would be such a fuss if she simply got up and went off, strolled down the garden or left to go indoors. It was like being a passenger on somebody else's ship, she thought, with no way of getting off. Or not until she had found Pierre. Poor old Marthe had been resigned long ago, she thought, sipping her coffee and looking at her sister's unoccupied chair. Besides, she was much too old, so perhaps it was just as well she had buried herself in a heap of tedious chores.

Marthe came back on to the verandah, slipping un-obtrusively into the chair she had left earlier. She gave her mother a little encouraging smile as she did so, to say that the little ones were safe, and had settled down.

75

Mama, she thought, was beginning to get that look which they had all come to recognize, when she seemed to let go of everything going on around her, as though she had lost some vital thread in an invisible maze. Her pale eyes had grown paler, now they had stopped looking, and turned almost stone blind. She glanced across at her sister, but Germaine was staring moodily at the table-cloth, fiddling with her coffee spoon.

'I'm getting on,' her stepfather was telling his visitor. 'Time to cultivate my own back garden.'

Michel suddenly got up, squeezed himself round the back of Germaine's chair, and went into the house without a word of apology or excuse. This time Marthe did catch her sister's eye, and Jean-Pierre looked anxiously down the table. But Claude gave no sign of having noticed his son's behaviour. He was in a relaxed mood as he shifted his bulk in the creaking chair, lit a cigarette and inhaled. A cloud of blue smoke drifted across the table, something all the women associated with masculinity. It hung on the air under the dense foliage, its faintly acrid odour overriding the scent of roses and any lingering smell of food.

'I'm always content to come back here.'

Here thought Jean-Pierre, I am leaving it, the only house and landscape I know, unfolding with time and season. Not a dream in which its contours do not figure, with the river flowing through it. Boating in summer, in winter skating, the varying moods of its unchanging flow. He had explored every bank and inlet, run wild over hillside and meadow, and lost himself in the process. Jean-Pierre fiddled with his beard rather self-consciously, thinking that perhaps the boy would stay lost, fishing and swimming, collecting botanical specimens and trapping hares long after he had left to continue his studies. It was an odd thought, and not one which Jean-Pierre was in a mood to pursue, but he could not help becoming conscious of it as he lifted his glass of plum brandy and leaned back in his chair, a man among men. He even accepted a cigar from Octave, glancing at his stepfather.

'The tide turns, the river rises or falls, and when I get back nothing looks the same. To say nothing of the weather.'

Claude's lifelong tussle with the forces of mutability, mostly too subtle for them to see, was a familiar theme, something they had all heard before. Jean-Pierre, thinking of his departure, and their boyhood, wished he might continue to do things with Michel, still sharing. It disturbed him that he had become so withdrawn and somehow passive. As if he did not know what to do with his life, thought Jean-Pierre, drawing on his cigar and feeling slightly sick.

Claude was telling the old joke against himself, the one about the time he had paid a farmer fifty francs to strip a tree of its leaves for what had begun as a winter landscape and hung around unfinished for too long.

'I was afraid he wouldn't do it, as the tree was down in a ravine. It took two men with very long ladders.'

Octave, the only one who had not heard it, smiled slightly. Jean-Pierre led the expected laughter, throwing himself forward so the table rocked, glasses chinked and tinkled against each other, trapped light in the water jug slipped and slithered like some thin silver fish. Alice

77

wiped tears from her eyes, but not of laughter. Germaine felt a hot surge run through her body and thought *oh Pierre Pierre Pierre* as she joined the chorus dutifully. I am hiding, she thought, in the thicket of their laughter, hearing their voices far away and hugging my secret to me in the dark place, crouching so I can smell the earth and the leaves and hear my own heart thumping.

'I'm getting too old to rush round like a fool. Better to sit still and let things come to you.'

Octave was leaning back in his chair, gold watch chain looped across the stomach of his waistcoat. 'My dear fellow,' he said, 'you still have the instincts of a hunter. But now you let the game come to you.' He pulled on his cigar and blew another smoke ring, something he had been doing to amuse his host's children for years. Just because they were now grown up seemed no good reason to stop. He gazed meditatively at the bluish loop of smoke as it hung on the air, thinking that though the hunter analogy was not his own it was nevertheless a good one, and might be developed in the future. For instance, the healthy pursuit of beauty in the arts as opposed to affectation, decadence, and posing. The smoke ring slackened, grew fuzzy at the edges, but kept its form for a surprisingly long time.

'We live in a luminous cloud of changing light, a sort of envelope. That is what I have to catch.'

He was startled, his eye still on the fading bluish wraith. It was not often that his friend expressed himself so fully in words, but now he had suddenly swept everything from his mind. He makes us see, he thought, seeing himself and Claude and the others sitting round the table in the garden in the middle of a luminous cloud of changing light which was now, here and now. And he felt the pulse of life quicken, as it took one of those sudden leaps which still made it worthwhile, in spite of everything. My dear old friend, he thought, lifting his glass of eau-de-vie.

'When I'm here,' Claude went on, 'I can get straight down to work without wasting time. In other places it always takes me a long time to get used to the landscape. I'm too busy grappling with it to notice the most important element of all. Here it is round me all the time, the luminous envelope.'

He noticed the dapple of light and shade behind Germaine's head coming through the dense foliage of the trellised roses. A protruding branch with an unopened bud at the tip threw a shadow on the shoulder of her blouse, and a halo of light caught the outer edges of her heavy pile of hair. But her face stayed in shadow, rose madder in tone, the features hardly visible, just smudges of darker shadow where the heavy hair overhung her forehead, and under the brows and the plump chin. Alice had looked like that, often, sitting absentminded at the end of a meal.

For a moment he forgot it was not his wife, looking at the pattern of light and shade, the slight tilt of the head. He had seen it before, this bulk of bluish shadow set off by an aura of light, the way a woman's hair and gown would sum up both fragility and mass, light and shadow, coalescing into a flowing form which pleased him. But sometimes now, time played tricks on him, and the woman sitting or posing had become a ghost whose line of light or shadow reminded him of somebody who had formed just such a pattern of light and falling shadow years ago, who now stood as if by some trick of the light, superimposed, shadow on shadow, blurring the edges of light. So his first wife had stood in his young stepdaughter's shadow, and now poor Suzanne had herself melted into air, leaving echoes, traces, in the faces which still sat round the table.

Alice had pushed back her chair and stood up. 'If you'll excuse me,' she murmured, drawing attention to her black gown, how it negated all things light and colourful in its texture. Her pale face, hollow with shadowy traces of misery and surrounded by hair which had gone quite white now, confirmed the message in the black cloth. It made them feel uneasy, guilty for a moment, because time went on and they had continued with their lives, enjoying it as now, regardless of its stopping.

Octave, who always observed a certain courteous formality with her, unhooked his thumbs from his waistcoat and stood up, scattering grey cigar ash. Marthe, looking up at her face and noticing the slight nervous twitch of the mouth, wondered whether she should follow her, but decided not to. One glance at her stepfather was enough: he already had the brooding, annoyed look she recognized. He disliked too much obvious fuss in front of visitors, and having his enjoyment spoilt. It was better to sit and look interested, even though at other times he would expect her to make her mother's welfare her first concern.

Alice had gone indoors without looking directly at anybody. There was a lull in the conversation, as each pursued his or her own thoughts, all somehow connected with the person who had just left, the dark privacy of her grief as each in his or her own way saw her walk through the empty rooms of the house, stirring its shadows, and step slowly, wearily, one step at a time up the steep narrow staircase to shut herself in her room. A tonic, thought Claude, as he heard her shut the door of her room. Beside him Jean-Pierre felt a sudden lift of spirit, and the word freedom occurred to him, since he was leaving. Poor mama, he thought, feeling happiness rise, with his own life just beginning.

The doorbell rang from the far side of the house, and Marthe, who had been about to ask the maids to clear the table, murmured 'Who can that be?' She glanced across at her sister and saw her flush darkly, her eyes intent on the open studio door, as though some apparition might walk through it. It's like an illness, thought Marthe, noticing the hectic flush and her eyes which saw nothing going on around her, dilated with some deep, dark inward vision which turned her blind. Even her hand shook as she lifted her empty coffee cup, still staring as though mesmerised at the doorway, but it was only the Abbé Toussaint who came through in his faded cassock, smiling shyly, ready to withdraw when he saw the visitor.

But Claude pointed to the empty chair at the end of the table and said casually, 'You know my friend Mirbeau?' whilst Marthe asked Marie to bring another cup and glass for the abbé. He sat down, still smiling shyly, elbows resting on the creaking cane, dusty black boots crossed under him at the ankles, and went on smiling with that benign, slightly nervous look, as if he had not heard the name of the visitor or it meant nothing particular to him.

'I'm afraid mama has gone up to rest,' Marthe told him, pouring his coffee. For the past year the whole family had relied on him to provide such comfort as the Church could offer, since she had always been rather pious, and most of them assumed that it was on her account he had come round now. With Mirbeau here, Claude did not wish to discuss Alice's state of mind, though it continued to worry him, so he simply poured Anatole a glass of eau-de-vie and pushed it down the table. An automobile, he was thinking, might do her more good than any notion so far.

The abbé leaned forward to take the glass, exposing a bony wrist under the black sleeve of his cassock.

'I wanted to see my pupil before he goes off,' he remarked, lifting his glass to Jean-Pierre in salute, his smile oddly vague because of the cast in his eye. He always seemed to be looking in two directions at once, or at no one in particular, less because of the defect in his vision than because he was nervously diffident, self-conscious of his bony limbs protruding from the shabby old cassock, folding his hands, tucking them away in the loose sleeves, doing much the same with his feet under the table.

'The abbé taught both the boys botany,' Claude explained to Octave. Mirbeau looked down the length of the table, quizzing the man with his most mocking smile. Anatole Toussaint's face, with the simian features and the receding hair smoothed back, still held the same vague, rather nervous smile.

'According to Darwin or Genesis?' he asked.

In the silence which followed Mirbeau's provocative remark everyone looked from him to the abbé, who seemed quite unruffled by this rapier thrust from a notorious scourge of the clergy. Like a great black bird which had alighted unasked at the lunch table, a bit nervous but unabashed, he glanced round the ring of faces. *Oh Lord* thought Marthe, and was thankful that mama had gone up to her room. But Jean-Pierre, who had known him since he was a small boy, out in the open fields, discussing specimens, watched him calmly. The abbé cleared his throat, glanced down at his clasped hands, and said diffidently:

'I believe the Church must come to terms with science, if it is to survive. To me the theory of evolution is the greatest miracle of all. I have studied it with interest. And after all,' he added, suddenly giving his monkey grin, 'seven days or seven million years—what is the difference in the mind of God, which is outside time?'

Octave looked thoughtful. 'Not bad,' he conceded. 'Though I should like to know what your bishop has to say about that.'

Toussaint's monkey grin grew broader, and the cast in his eye looked almost sly, as though he was conscious of looking in more than one direction.

'Luckily our bishop, like most bishops, leaves us very much to our own devices in this village.' His grin took in Jean-Pierre, who smiled back happily, feeling his spirit lift with sudden elation at the thought of going out into the world, full of so much promise and excitement. It was partly the wine, he knew, but it was also more.

83

Quietly mocking, sure of himself now, the abbé continued: 'Or he might have had the young men of this household excommunicated for interfering with the laws of nature, and God.'

'Michel and I used to try our hand at cross-fertilization,' laughed Jean-Pierre. 'With varying success. Though we did produce a very handsome poppy.'

'It almost took over the entire garden,' grunted Claude, amused, in a thoroughly good humour.

'*Papaver Moneti*. But to tell the truth,' said Toussaint, 'it was a bit of an accident. In other words, an act of God. Some of their own experiments were quite disastrous.'

He was relaxed now, at ease, knowing himself among friends. He uncrossed his ankles, unfolded his hands and said yes, perhaps he would have another glass of eau-de-vie. Just a small one. Mirbeau, recognising a botanist and keen gardener under his black cloth, was inclined to forgive him for it. Besides, good food and drink in pleasant surroundings took the edge off his opinions now he had turned fifty: his digestion could not cope with too much. As for Claude, it was all one to him anyhow. Everything.

'Come and see my orchids,' he said, to Octave and the abbé in turn, pushing back his chair.

It was the signal for the lunch party to break up. There was a general pushing back of chairs, a brushing down of crumbs and ash from clothing. Marthe walked along the verandah and tapped on the glass of the kitchen door, so the servants would know they could clear the table, then went indoors. Jean-Pierre watched his stepfather

84

strolling towards the greenhouse with Mirbeau and Toussaint, both now pausing to discuss a plant with each other. *The old magician*, he thought, then suddenly remembered a social engagement in the village and jumped up from the table. Germaine lingered for a moment, idle and uncertain, before going indoors.

Eight

Shadows lengthened across the garden, creeping up on glowing patches of colour still in sunlight. They fell slanting from pergolas and pyramids across gravel paths and flowerbeds, gathered under shrubs and began to spill slowly. Trees now engulfed portions of the garden in mysterious pools of shadow where dark stirred on dark, liquid indigo moving on colours of leaf shadow to form darker hues and shades. Where lawn and flowerbeds still lay in sunshine the light had changed to a soft golden luminosity, it had an edge to it, a glow, and insects hovering above bright flowers were lit up like jewels in an illuminated showcase. Down by the lily pond the willow tree at the far end stood in a blaze of yellow sunlight, turning its leaves pale, almost without colour, stirring fingers of light, whilst under the bridge the water now looked darker, deeper, a dragonfly moved from sunlight to shadow and the line of poplars had become a wall of blue shadow between afternoon and evening, sunlight and shadow. The sun stood high above them, but even now the light was filtering through their tips, sloping to catch leaf and branch through a growing thicket of darkness, glancing off the topmost leaves of bamboo whose roots were buried deep in damp earth heavy with night. Here the pond ended amongst marshy undergrowth which hid the second, gurgling sluice.

My darling child, wrote Alice in her journal, and stopped, conscious of the silence around her, of whispering words in an empty room. She stared at the lines she had just formed on the page, and put down her pen for a moment, to rest her head in her hands. It was absurd, speaking to the dead, whilst the walls of the room seemed to close in on her, and outside the sounds of another summer mocked her foolish endeavor. But with her eyes closed like this in the soft hollow of her palms it was possible, somewhere, quite close to her, Suzanne stood breathing softly, she could almost hear the swish of her gown, not the sound of wind sighing in the trees outside, but as if, were she to lift her head without warning, she might suddenly make out the shadow of her outline, against the window or flitting across the far side of the room.

87

Nothing is lost, she whispered, before her grief came back in a huge black wave to wash over her, drowning everything. It must all somehow co-exist, past and present, living and dead, but now they were just words, dry and empty. Your children are growing up, she whispered, knowing how growth obscured everything in time.

Farther down the valley Theodore listened to the steady trot of the horse's hooves and finally made up his mind. All of it, the familiar road, walls and trees, sun alternating with shade as the trap rumbled on helped to confirm him in his decision. He owed it to his children, who had been born here, and who had never known anything outside this village. He owed it to Marthe, who had done so much for them. Besides, it was too late to expect success in the States, even if he wanted to go back, and he was not sure that he really did. He was settled now, and, at fifty, hardly getting any younger. As he watched the river landscape unwinding beyond the road he felt as though its continuity had become part of him, winding its way through his life as the river did through pasture and copse, marsh and meadow, now it was lost to sight, now seen again as a distant gleam. I shall never be a really good painter, he told himself, perhaps for the first time, but now he had admitted as much he also knew that living in Claude's aura and shadow meant more to him than anything. It was what had first attracted him to Suzanne, and by marrying her sister he would ensure the tie held. He caught his first glimpse of the church spire through the line of trees. He would leave his portmanteau at home, wash and change his shirt, then stroll over to his father-in-law-'s house. Perhaps he should have a word with Marthe first, then talk to the old man. Ever since he had stepped on to the train at Paris he had been wanting to ask him what he thought of the way they had hung his stuff at the Exhibition.

Marthe shook the last crumbs from the bread basket on to the gravel path below, but a few bits fell on the steps. It was suddenly very quiet, no sounds coming from the house, nobody in the garden. All she could hear was a wasp droning near the table, and something else, distant, like a very faint sigh rustling through the universe. She stood very still and it seemed to move through the dark foliage of the yew trees, breathe through the heavy hanging creeper over the verandah. Down below it shimmered in the pale sunlit mass of the willow tree by the pond, she was sure of it, though she could not hear it.

It struck Marthe that this was the first moment during the day when she had been by herself, and she found this curious, she knew the moment to be unusual, possibly precious, but did not know what to do about it. The children were asleep, mama was resting, nobody was within earshot as she stood at the top of the verandah steps looking down at the empty garden, still holding the bread basket. Who are you, Marthe, something inside her had been waiting not just hours but years to ask, without finding the proper respite: who are you, Marthe, and what do you really need? She ran her finger along the rough surface of the wickerwork. Now that she had time to think about it she did not really mind the possibility of Germaine marrying, and she had always known that she was likely to be the one left behind at home. She had been a bit jealous throughout lunch, but only because she envied her for being so sure, for knowing just what would make her happy, and not because she would have liked to marry Pierre Sisley, or anybody else, come to that. All her life she had been doing things because they needed doing, and she was around to do them. She tried to think what it would be like to do something, anything, from choice. What would she, Marthe, choose to do?

A small bird hopped warily along the bottom step of the verandah, then stopped to listen, its head cocked to one side. Marthe knew she had only to make a slight movement and it would never take the crumbs which lay so near it. Knowing she could startle it, she stood quite still, watching. Something about its cockiness, the angled alert head and round moving eye, made her want to smile as though it had been a child, trying so hard to be cunning in a world too large for it. She wanted to laugh out loud, but stood, merely smiling, as it moved forward, hop by cautious hop, and its sharp round eye took in the known universe, which perhaps included her, Marthe, standing round and fat on the verandah, with nothing to do and the family bread basket in her hand.

The bird took the crumb and flew off, so suddenly she had no idea where it had gone to. Oh well, she thought, looking down at the empty verandah step, and turned to put the bread basket back on the table. And then, seeing the litter of cups, plates and glasses it occurred to her that all this should have been cleared away an hour ago. Where was everybody? She walked along the verandah and tapped on the glass of the kitchen door, trying to peer through the part not covered by thin cotton drapes. It was very dark inside, after the bright sunlight of the garden, and at first she could see nothing except shadows and her own face reflected in the pane. Cook would have gone by now, she knew, until it was time to start again for supper, but that left Marie and the new girl.

As her eyes got accustomed to the dark she saw first the milky glass shade of the hanging lamp, then the glint of copper pans and the heavy iron range to the left of the door and, last of all, the two of them sitting at the table in the centre of the room. They were deep in conversation, Marthe saw, now that her eyes had adjusted, though she had to put her hand against the glass to cut out her own reflection. So deep in conversation that they did not hear her tap on the pane or notice her figure darkening the verandah door. Their two heads were almost touching as they leaned across the kitchen table, and she wondered what Marie could possibly find to say to a young girl who had only been in the house for a week and knew nothing about anything, and what could be so intensely absorbing. For a moment she felt excluded, for a few fleeting seconds she would have given anything to be part of that intimacy, share what they had to say to each other, their chairs tipping forward and elbows propped on the table. But then she tapped on the glass once more, sharply, something peremptory about it, and they turned their heads and saw her, eyes round and startled like two hares in a field, she thought, and pushed back their chairs in haste.

Marthe walked back along the verandah and down the steps, scarcely glancing at the table with its neglected litter. She felt as though a door had closed behind her, and that she had somehow shut it. But she had thought of Marie as almost one of the family, not one to sit gossiping with a young chit who had just been taken on. She walked down the gravel path, stopping to look at clumps of bright flowers, but without seeing them. Of course she was doing her duty, as mama would have her do. But all her life she had felt closer to the servants, or some of them, than anybody else in the household. Somebody like Marie, who was solid and sensible, good-humoured and took everything in her stride, she would rather sit with Marie and talk than anybody.

The abbé stood chatting for a few moments at the door to the hothouse and said he would see himself out. Such extraordinary colours and shapes, he thought, quite failing to notice mademoiselle Marthe standing only a yard or two away as he trudged up the gravel path, who would ever have imagined that he would be privileged to see them with his own eyes, orchideæ of such splendour growing in front of his very eyes, here in his own village. How very different from the pale flat artists' impressions in the reference books, which was all he had ever expected to see in his lifetime. And what a charming man Mirbeau was, a real gardening enthusiast, whatever his political opinions. The two of them had had a most interesting discussion on propagating techniques as they wandered round the hothouse, and his knowledge was evidently considerable.

It was only when he was outside in the lane, with a stray dog sniffing round the dusty hem of his cassock and the sun in his eyes that he remembered why, after seeing madame standing at her daughter's grave at dawn, he had decided to pay a call this afternoon. Once more, he thought, he had failed in his duty and found instead pleasure and personal satisfaction, it was always the same when he came to this household. Still with the sun in his eyes the abbé began to walk slowly down the rutted lane. Perhaps it was a sin, he thought, kicking a stone in his path as he passed windows shuttered against the sun, giving the whole street a deserted look. But if so, he argued, he had hardly been in a state of grace before the painter settled in the village. He had never told anyone, not even in confession, just how far the black shadow of doubt had taken him when he first arrived in the village. Now that *had* been a sin, he concluded, beside which his little sin of self-indulgence hardly counted. And if a little sin drives out a greater the mind of God must rejoice, he thought, giving his simian grin into the bright afternoon sun. As he told madame Alice when she worried about her husband's lack of faith, the house of God has many mansions. He had told Mirbeau much the same thing while they discussed the variation of plant species in the orchid house, and he had not disagreed.

He reached the far end of the village and stopped, as he often did, to take in the wide view of the valley stretching out below him. From outside his church he could see long colourful fields running down to the river, which gleamed fitfully under the line of hillslope beyond. The view had hardly changed in all the years he had lived here, though now the village was full of foreigners and some of the locals had given up cultivating the higher, rougher ground to find easier ways of making a profit. Anatole Toussaint looked down at the fields lying in a golden haze of summer heat and thought that it would soon be harvest time once more. It had been a good spring and summer, but he contemplated the harvest to come with mixed feelings: it reminded him too much of death, of smoke in the air, leaves turning yellow, bleak winter days with a mist on the horizon and a grey sky stretching to infinity. Cold months during which he was dismally conscious of his own crop growing in the soil round the church, each year bringing more headstones and high grey crosses, stark as the leafless trees.

Birth, marriage and death, he thought, turning round as he heard the sound of a horse and trap approaching. As it slowed down he recognized Claude's bereaved son-in-law, the American, so different now from the gay, rather flamboyant figure who had married Suzanne a few years back. He had aged, grown thin, something defeated about him, though he wore much the same clothes and affected the same manner, wearily, like a mimic who knows what is expected of him.

Theodore leaned down to say a few words, and though he was smiling bravely Anatole noticed a shadow in the eyes even now, fleeting, disturbed, which had nothing to do with the shadow cast by his wide-brimmed hat.

'I'm just back from Paris,' he announced, a man of the world who had decided to turn his back on it. 'Have you seen my little family?'

Nine

'*I thought you'd never come,*' said Jimmy. '*Can I get up now?*'

He had been listening for the sound of Marthe's footsteps outside in the corridor for what seemed an eternity. Footsteps had come and gone, ignoring him, almost mocking him as the hollow sound died away, till he felt that the afternoon must have passed without him.

On the far side of the railway track the two men had begun to cross the curved bridge over the lily pond. Octave walked slightly behind his host, who had been leading the way, showing off a new plant, indicating an effect, an unusual vista, or pausing to examine buds hidden in foliage.

'It's been a remarkable year for roses,' he said, turning round at the foot of the bridge. 'Didn't you find?'

By now the bank of climbing roses looked almost white in the oblique, falling light, a mass of slightly crumpled petals.

Octave said nothing, not wishing to disturb their mood by mentioning his greenfly, which in turn reminded him of a terrible row with his wife, and its uneasy aftermath. He sighed. That was *his* home. While this...

Claude had stopped at the high point of the wooden arc. He always did. When guests were taken on a tour of the garden they lingered longest here, and a hush fell as the conversation died. Even though Octave had been here often, the two men rested their hands on the rail and stood for a while looking down at the water, their own reflections almost immersed in the darker reflection cast by the bridge itself and the high trees behind, so that only their heads were outlined in the light of shining water farther out. Farther still, each water lily had become a curved cup of glowing colour resting on a flat saucer of indigo shadow. And at the far end of the pool, catching the full afternoon sun, the willow trees stood in a blaze of shimmering light, long leaves trembling, falling in a cascade of palest green and gold. Halfway across the pond fell the slanting edge between sun and shadow, dividing the world. Insects flew from one to the other, carrying light on their wings. A downy seed pappus floated by with sunlight in its cobweb texture. Yet even now the clear cool shadows of the water reflected patches of the summer sky, deep as it was distant, as though high noon gleamed through the dark glass of dusk in a wondrous duplicity of hours.

Octave sensed a brooding silence in his host, which he did not like to disturb. Behind him he heard water running through the sluice, gurgling back into the stream from which it had been drawn.

'You should have heard the fuss when I started building it.' Claude dropped his half-smoked cigarette, eyes still intent on the water. 'I had to get planning permission to divert the stream. The locals seemed to think I might poison all their livestock downstream.'

Octave chortled: it was a story after his own heart, showing, as it did, the stupidity of peasants, bureaucrats, petty officials...

Lily had been watching the strips of dusty light falling from the closed shutters, wondering for perhaps the thousandth time why the sunlight should be full of dancing motes, gleaming and moving, when the rest of the air seemed quite empty. Now, hearing footsteps, whispers, she closed her eyes very tight and tried to make her breathing sound even. She heard the swish of a skirt, a floorboard creak, and then Marthe whisper loudly: 'Your sister seems to be fast asleep.' Lily lay for a moment, unable to control the grin, trying to move her hand over her mouth very slowly, then suddenly leapt up into the air shouting 'No I'm not... I'm not asleep at all.' Once she started bouncing up and down on the mattress she wanted to go on, feeling the air moving round her bare

97

arms and the walls leaping wildly about. Suppose her head hit the ceiling, she thought, catching sight of her aunt as she came down. 'Now now,' she was saying, 'mustn't get over-excited,' putting out an arm to catch hold of her, but Lily wanted to go higher and faster, so that her pulse raced and she was tingling all over, go on till she was quite out of breath.

'Show off,' said Jimmy, with dismissive contempt in his voice. 'I knew you weren't really asleep.'

Lily pulled a face and started making stupid noises with her tongue out: yayaya. Marthe made a grab at her and gave a little slap on her bare upper arm.

'Cry baby,' said Jimmy impassively, as the tears started to roll down her face.

Claude and Octave were halfway down the meadow when they heard the local train approaching through the valley, growing louder as it chuffed and rattled along the track and momentarily vanished behind a fringe of trees, except for its head of steam which drifted upward and hung for a while, before dissipating into nothing.

'I want to see the train,' said Lily, struggling under her aunt's hand.

'Don't be silly,' said Marthe, tugging the comb through her thick dark hair, 'you've seen it dozens of times before. Besides, you want to look beautiful, don't you?'

'No I don't,' said Lily.

The sound of the train died away. Octave was in his shirt sleeves now, his jacket slung over one shoulder, a long feathery grass helm in the corner of his mouth, thick grass swishing against his legs. Now that the train had gone the meadow hummed with the chirrup of hidden insects. He disturbed a butterfly which hovered.

'What's more,' said Claude, catching up with him. 'They wanted to build a factory on this bit of land. I had to buy them off.'

A cloud shadow moving over the grass turned it suddenly amethyst, the light of buttercups went out like candles as the shadow of amethyst moved across them, poppy heads died as slow-glowing embers, the grass has become a shuddering slipstream of cool blues and greys, clover-coloured, deep and mobile as the river beyond.

'These people,' he added, 'don't understand the value of what they've got.'

Ten

Marthe was sewing on the verandah when the doorbell rang on the far side of the house. Probably Theodore come to fetch his children, she thought, and went on stitching Lily's new pinafore. In which case he would come straight through to the garden and surprise them. Both of them were oddly still now, Lily slouched in a cane chair with her eyes half-closed and her legs swinging, Jimmy idling with a stick on the bottom step of the verandah, humming some sort of monotonous tune to himself. The droning threnody had begun to fill the air and her own thoughts till she could think of nothing but the warm air and her own lassitude and wind stirring the Virginia creeper. It would be a good thing for him to come now, for she had run out of things to do with them, and they did not seem in the mood to do anything on their own.

Marthe twisted the white thread, snipped the end off and looked up to see Marie standing at her elbow in the studio doorway.

'Some sort of gipsy,' said Marie, moving from one foot to the other, her heavy weight almost blocking the doorway.

'Well, give him a few sous. You know where mama keeps the change.'

Marthe made Lily stand up and held the unfinished pinafore against her for size.

'He's not begging exactly,' said Marie slowly, 'he's selling.' Her eye caught Lily's two dark ones, staring at her above Marthe's busy prodding hands, and a broad sly smile spread across her face. 'He's selling toys.'

It was as though an electric charge had gone through both children. Jimmy leapt to his feet and up the steps, hardly giving Marie time to move aside before he was stampeding through the house with his sister following behind. Lily had been slower to react, and first had to disentangle herself from the half-made pinafore. She got scratched by a pin as she made her escape, but it hardly hurt while she was running. She could hear Marie laugh behind her and her aunt calling for her not to go so fast as though running was dangerous or impolite, she was never quite sure which, but by this time she was through the echoing studio and up the steps only just behind

Jimmy, and she saw him as he stood framed in the doorway with the dusty sunlight of the lane behind him.

He had a tray slung from his shoulders with all kinds of things on it, little leather purses and whistles shaped like birds and windmills that went round on sticks but her eyes were held by the cluster of balloons floating in the air so that the air itself was like the colours of the rainbow, red and blue and green. And because they hung on the air with their strings quite straight, gently bouncing into each other, the man looked as though he could be lifted into the air and float up into the sky at any moment.

'Well,' said Theodore, seeing the pedlar at the door and both his children standing wide-eyed and with their mouths open on the threshold, and he fished in his pocket for loose change. Marthe had come up behind them holding her purse and before he remembered his decision he noticed how unlike his wife she was, stout and plain. She flushed when she saw him standing unexpectedly behind the pedlar, and laughed, and now he saw his good-hearted sister-in-law fumbling with her purse in the doorway. The image he had seen a moment ago went out of his mind, leaving only a faint feeling of unease, almost physical, a sense of something not quite right which he had often felt on finishing a painting. Then, as now, he could only ignore it. Marthe *was* a little flushed from the heat, of course. 'No no, let me,' he said, picking out some coins from his palm to give to the pedlar, and the gesture soothed him, the uneasy fluttering in his chest began to subside as he paid him off.

'Look, can we talk?' he asked, taking his sister-in-law

by the elbow as she shut the door on the vagabond. Luckily his children had scarcely noticed him, hypnotised by their newly acquired playthings. Jimmy was running through to the kitchen, blowing shrilly on his bird whistle and his daughter, well, she looked slightly awestruck, as though she was walking on air.

Lily held on to the string and walked very cautiously down the polished wooden steps into the studio, taking one step at a time, then pausing to look up. The fact that she wanted to keep looking up at the balloon, when she knew she should be looking down at where her feet were going made everything much more precarious. It was as though her relationship with the floor had become tenuous, the balloon pulled upward, bumping into things, and as she tugged on the string, trying to control it, she might stumble and fall or find herself suddenly strung up and floating as she did in dreams, skimming through the space between high shadowy ceiling and the waxed wooden floor.

Her grandmother was sitting in the studio, writing a letter at her bureau. She glanced up, saw the balloon, and smiled.

'Well,' she said, and went on writing.

Lily could not remember the last time grandmama had smiled. She stood near the bureau and waited for something more to happen. Surely it was momentous, this here and now in which she stood, swaying slightly, looking up at the balloon which swung to her motion. But the nib went on scratching, and her tired old head with its burden of white hair did not look up. It had always been hard to win her attention, since she was mostly sad. Lily looked curiously at the brown specks on the back of her hands for a bit, pondering the opaque mystery of being so very old, sighed, and gave up.

Above her head the balloon looked oddly dull. It was still bright red, of course, up in the shadows amongst the rows of pictures, but it no longer shone as it had done, with the sky showing through it in the doorway. Behind its round shape the figure of her mother stood on the hillside as though the bright summer wind was about to carry her off, and only the slanting shadow of her parasol held her with her feet on the ground. It was mama, but mama as an angel in heaven. Just as she had been told. And at night, with her eyes closed, or when she prayed, she saw her just like this, her face lost in shadow, bluish wings coming from her shoulders and her white dress blowing in the summer meadow, as though her soft glowing figure was going to merge into the nacreous summer sky. But because her face was blurred and indistinct in the shadow of the parasol, Lily could not now remember it.

Puddles of light shone along the wood floor. The shadow of a leaf moved. The garden was framed in the door to the verandah, lambent with green and gold. Lily turned towards it, carefully holding on to the string. She put her foot into a pool of sunlight, and it lit up the bottom of her pinafore. Leaf shadows moved across her, she felt as though she was swimming through light and shadow, dazzled so she could not see where her foot was going now. But then she saw Marie standing in the doorway which led through to the kitchen.

'Well,' she said, wiping her hands on the corner of her apron. 'Isn't that something.' And she looked at the balloon as though she had never seen anything quite like it.

'I think I'll take it outside,' Lily said, cautiously drawing in the string so it would not hit the lintel or catch in the overhanging foliage, and all the time she could feel Marie's eyes at her back, watching her go. Lily felt that moving through the vision of grownups was decidedly odd, like being in and out of focus by turn. She did not know which she minded most, being ignored, or being watched as though she was performing.

But once she was outside she forgot about being watched. She always did, if only because the garden was full of secret hiding places. She counted down the verandah steps, felt her shoes crunch solid gravel, and looked up. The balloon was luminous now, slowly she let out the string until it had reached its full extent, watched it rise upward, then sway slightly against the sky. She stood for a moment in the shadow of the yew trees, and here the sky looked very blue but far away, the air almost mauve now through its coloured transparency, then started to walk down the gravel path until she reached the sunlight. This time when she looked up she almost could not see anything, her eyes so blinded and dazzled by the sunlight that she saw spots swimming across her vision.

Auguste was kneeling on one of the paths, planting out seedlings from a wooden tray, beside him a wheelbarrow full of dead flowers and weeds. Lily walked past him with her head held back so she could look up, hearing her feet on the gravel. It was like being in two places at once, stretched long and thin as the piece of string she was holding. Auguste sat back on his heels and smiled, his skin quite brown with earth and sun. 'Well,' he said, watching her go.

Lily started to run, round and round the flowerbeds, the red balloon bobbing behind her, tugging in the slipstream, but each time she stopped, gasping and out of breath, it was up there again, serenely floating against the sky. She sat down on a bench, swinging her legs, and watched it. Looking *through* it was the secret, she decided, if you just looked at it the balloon seemed rather dull, a matt surface which would begin to wrinkle, its navel tied with twine. But its red transparency changed everything, the quality of vision, like closing her eyes against the sunlight, and seeing bright red through the lids. She closed her eyes to find out what would come inside.

When she opened them Jimmy stood on the footpath, watching her. The sun struck his fair hair, but his eyes looked dark and determined. He had stopped blowing his bird whistle, which stuck out of his trouser pocket.

'Let me hold it.'

Lily shook her head, dumb but wary. She could feel a slight flutter in her chest as her heart began to beat a little more quickly.

'I'll let you have a go of this.'

Jimmy offered her the bird whistle in the palm of his hand.

'No.'

Lily slid off the bench and began to walk hurriedly through the garden, not looking at things, trying to hear Jimmy's footsteps following behind. But she would not look round. He might think she was scared of him. She stopped by the gate to the footbridge across the railway track and heard voices, sounding like grandpapa and his visitor, so she stood in the hot sunlight without moving for what seemed a long time until she saw their heads coming up above the top of the bridge, grandpapa with his face in shadow under the straw hat pointing to something beyond the house, his hand half concealed by the cambric cuff too long for the sleeve of his jacket, his friend pausing to look in the required direction, thumbs in his waistcoat, but frowning slightly, as though he could not quite make it out from so far away.

'Well,' said Octave, seeing the little girl at the bottom of the steps, and he jokingly knocked the balloon with his hand to make it bounce and sway. 'Where did that come from?'

'A gipsy.' Lily fell into step with him, trying to take two steps to his one. She felt safe now, though she could still see her brother in his white sailor suit hovering within the periphery of her vision.

Octave turned round to wink at his host. 'You see— what would we do without gipsies and vagabonds?'

Claude grunted something, pulling at the shrivelled head of a peony.

'Your father back yet?' he asked Jimmy, suddenly close to him.

'He's talking to aunt Marthe about something.'

The slow procession moved between the flowerbeds, pausing when Claude stopped to examine a bloom or show his friend a newly purchased specimen which was doing well in his soil. Lily had dropped back to take grandpapa's hand, skipping alongside his heavy slow tread. Sometimes she jumped on his shadow, and laughed, coming back to swing on his hand. They saw clusters of white phlox, big bushes of hydrangea shading from pink through mauve to sky blue, and grandpapa had to shoo a bumble bee off with his hat. So when Jimmy asked in a loud voice if he could hold her balloon for a while she gave it to him without a word, partly because she did not mind, but also because it was impossible to refuse with grandpapa listening, as Jimmy knew. Grownups were always going on about selfish conduct, and it was worst in public.

The little party moved on. Auguste came by with his wheelbarrow. A large amber butterfly with black marks on its wings like two eyes settled on a poppy. The poppy, thought Lily, had petals rather like crumpled wings, too fragile not to fall off the slender hairy stalks. Her grandfather and the visitor with the gold watch chain across his waistcoat had stopped to discuss a small green shrub with no flowers on at all, and she was scuffing the gravel with her foot when she heard a shriek and looked up. Her balloon had begun to float upward, by the time she saw it, it was already high above the ginkgo tree, as they watched it rose above the level of the yew trees beyond, now it was higher than the house, up above the hillside, a bright red sphere with its dangling string, growing smaller as it climbed, higher and higher, the light shining on it, until it was only a tiny red dot, and then nothing, just high high, light and air in which she could imagine it still rising.

Nobody spoke for a while. They had all been standing with their heads thrown back, staring into the empty sky.

'Will it go up for ever?' Lily asked in a hushed voice. She was awestruck by what had happened, and also a bit proud, because it was her balloon that had done this wondrous thing.

'Of course,' said Octave, smoothing his hair.

'It might drift,' said Claude, putting his straw hat back on. 'In which case lots of people will see it, all over the country.'

Lily thought about this, imagining surprised eyes looking up into the sky, in unknown countryside stretching beyond here. It was only after she had thought about this, and the blue sky had been empty for some time, that her loss occurred to her. Jimmy had let go of her balloon. Jimmy ought to be made to give her his bird whistle, but nobody had told him to do so. Lily brooded, but did not know how to come out with it.

She saw her father coming down the verandah steps with aunt Marthe, both of them smiling, but awkwardly, as if they were unsure about something in coming out now, from the house, to meet them.

'Did you see the balloon go up?' called Jimmy, running forward to his father, who just said 'Really?' in a vague sort of way, as though he had noticed nothing in particular, but did not like to admit it.

'I've lost my balloon,' Lily announced in an accusing voice to nobody in particular.

'No you haven't.' It was the man with the moustache and the gold watch chain across his chest. He had not spoken directly to her before. Now he put his hand on her head and leaned forward. There was an amused ironic look in his eyes, as he said confidentially, so she could feel his breath on her ear: 'That's the only way to keep a balloon—by letting it go. Didn't you know that?'

The others laughed. Lily, staring into Octave's smiling eyes, was not sure if he, and they, were laughing at her. Everything was very confusing, she thought, not knowing whether to laugh too, letting resentment go. She saw her father turn to aunt Marthe and touch her elbow. Jimmy was kicking at some gravel, refusing to meet her eye, his bird whistle safely tucked out of sight in his trouser pocket, which bulged. Her grandfather put his hand on her shoulder.

'He's right, you know,' he said gruffly, and she trusted the tone of his voice. Leaning against his trouser leg, she heard him add: 'You wait and see.'

Eleven

Five o'clock. The top of the willow tree still shone in green light.
The same light was visible on the slope beyond the house,
and on the open fields between the railway track and the
river. But the water of the lily pond was sunk in cool
shadow, and only the air above it still gleamed fitfully
in the slanting light, soft and tenuous as it came through
the trees, playful as mist on the substance of shadow
below, which it could not disturb. It was as though a
tangible split had occurred between sunlight, shadow and
substance, and now earth and water were sinking into

themselves, taking leave of the sky. Dragonflies and a swarm of midges could still cross the divide, hovering in the air above the depth of shadow, catching the fitful gleam, but the lilies had begun to close up their colours as the water darkened and the sky withdrew from its surface and stood high above the trees.

Light still played on the foliage in the garden, but the shadows within it grew dark. It threw long shadows on to footpaths and flowerbeds, highlighting pools of yellow gravel, clumps of snapdragon and marigold. It spilled on patches of open lawn, which looked more bright and inviting than at any time during the day, because of the surrounding shadows. It glowed in the tops of rose-bushes, making their blooms incandescent for a time, just before the petals began to drop. It gleamed on the upper windows of the house, fading the curtains and covers of empty bedrooms. Even the dull slate roof shone with a mauve tint. But the light visible on the slope behind the house seems to have drawn it in, brought it nearer, and though the upper windows gleam gold the floor below is sunk in shadow, a tide is slowly rising which has submerged the living rooms and the trellised verandah, now the yew trees, then the rosebush pyramids.

Down by the lily pond Claude stood for a moment, put a match to his cigarette, and allowed his eyes to wander from the remote reflections still visible in the surface of the water to the willow trees almost submerged in blue shadow, their tops sunlit. He felt as though the world he knew was drawing away from him, that he could hold neither shadow nor light, which had changed to something far more mysterious. The remaining sunlight had detached itself from the shadows, and now it clung to the very texture of things, leaf flower grass, had become part of it, even of wood or stone, so that those things which it still lit had become insubstantial, luminous from within. He strolled along the grass verge, saying his habitual goodbye to shrubs and trees now glowing in a final incandescence he had not captured, not yet. He had been wrong to think of light as a veil, playful and shimmering, between him and solid things. That was how a young man saw things, in midsummer, and at midday. But now, especially in the early morning and in the evening, he saw it for the illusion it was. He had to look through things now, since nothing is solid, to show how light and those things it illumines are both transubstantial, both tenuous.

Tomorrow he would go back to the river and make a new beginning. Just as each day is a new beginning, he thought, stopping to look at his rosebush now incandescent in the afternoon light, its blooms about to dissolve into the surrounding atmosphere, to melt into air as he had seen stonework do. He touched a petal on the burning bush and thought of the extraordinary theory of atoms, and how it was not unlike what he could see for himself: each day light playing defining and transforming what would otherwise be merely grey amorphous matter, whether leaf, water or rock. As though with each dawn the miracle of creation was recreated with the coming of first light. Beginning with the calm blues and greys he would find on the river.

He saw his wife coming down the path to find him, and knew she had something on her mind. As she took his arm and they strolled round the pond together he had a sense of well-being, knowing that he had improved both house and garden these past few years, added the hothouse, purchased the second studio next door, and each season gave him the opportunity to improve every inch of ground.

'It's absurd,' he said, 'since the boy has neither money nor prospects.' They turned under the willow tree to continue walking in the sun, and were caught by a dazzle of oblique light coming through the trees beyond the arc of the bridge. He saw the colours coming from it, each leaf and branch a prism deflecting its purity, but Alice walked with her head bowed, watching the path and their feet moving in rhythm. she did not argue with him, but tried to absorb his words, to justify them. In a few months, he went on, Germaine would have forgotten all about him, though he could hardly forbid him the house. And if not, one might send her away for a few weeks. Alice hid her uneasiness.

The sunlight was receding beyond the trees, and with it her youngest daughter's immediate hope of happiness, the feverish glow which had been burning in her, flushing her cheeks through the day and making her skin tingle right through to her fingertips. She did not know it yet, or rather, she did know, since from the beginning fear had been part of her nervous elation, and from early morning her sense of joy had been heightened by apprehension, not of anything in particular, though she knew that Claude's word was law, but of all things.

Through shadows moving on shadow, on the far side of the lily pond, slid ghosts from the past, Camille's thin form wavering among the trees, in spite of all he could now do for the living. It was an unspoken thing between them, but they both felt it, those uneasy shadows lurking just out of sight in the evening, and at nightfall, it kept them from speaking of things which might otherwise have been fully discussed, and changed. It was all so long ago, she thought, as a sudden gust of wind chilled her, and sent a shower of dying petals across their path and fluttering down the front of her black dress, but nothing could be changed now, and besides, she respected his wish to shield the living from so much suffering. Was it possible, she wondered, shivering slightly, knowing that each day brought its portion. She lifted her head and saw the line of poplars shimmering in the dying gust of wind. So long ago, she thought, but not for us. For us it is now, always.

Across the fields the last train of the day rattled down the narrow track, its engine chuffing steadily. A short shrill whistle echoed through the valley at a certain moment, it broke the rhythm but was part of it, since the timing never varied, sounds so much part of the rhythm of their lives that those who lived in the valley heard it, and did not hear it. Jimmy, standing at an upstairs window, did hear it, and it set him thinking of going away, far away, as far as Ohio. Father had come from there, many years ago. Lily heard it too, and imagined the people sitting in the carriages who would suddenly look out and catch sight of a red balloon. But nobody else heard it, not really, only as they took in so many familiar sounds. The servants were preparing the evening meal,

a bit rushed, having somehow got behind with everything. Marthe was trying to imagine herself as Theodore's
wife, and hoping mama would not mind. It was not, after
all, as though she was leaving the village. Claude never
heard anything when he had something to see, now two
white butterflies circling round each other in the falling
light, and though Alice heard a train it was the one in
which she had started to give birth to Jean-Pierre when
she fled from Paris to escape her husband's creditors. And
now he was grown up too, the last of her brood, going
off to study, a young man with a thick growth of beard
hiding his features: she still found it odd.

The sky had begun to change colour, completely, a
totality hardly visible from within the garden, closed in
by trees and shrubs. But the abbé, outside his church
once more, saw the whole of the western horizon turning
bright pink and gold, while above his head a solitary
skylark rose higher and higher, its clear chirruping song
the only sound in the whole world. It was difficult to
believe that all would not be right with God's creation
at moments such as this. Theodore, walking from his
own house to dine with his father-in-law, noticed how
windows caught the redgold light, and felt that everything was settled now, as far as his own future was con-
cerned. Things would go on much as before, and since
the children were used to Marthe, telling them would be
no problem. Only another war, he had told her, would
make him leave Europe now, and she had smiled with
relief, since the best people felt the notion of war had
become absurd. Mirbeau had said as much, only the other

day. A dog zigzagged across his path, stopping to sniff both edges of the lane in turn.

Down by the lily pond Claude also saw the sky turn rose and gold, taking colour from the trees, making the thicket of bamboo darker, and more dense. A couple of swallows dipped and swung, as though for the joy of it, finding their freedom in the space above and around him. The air was soft now, slightly misty, everything, leaves, fences, the house, touched with gold. The four poplar trees across his horizon had turned to pillars of flame, as though the world were burning in a silent conflagration, reflected in the glowing sky. The element of fire had taken hold, he thought, but tomorrow it will begin all over again, I will find a world cool with blue and grey, damped down with dew, and the show will play through once more. I have nothing to fear, he thought, in the time left. This is enough, more than enough, it will finish with me long before I have finished with it.

Seven o'clock, and now light shone red on the lily pond, and pools of indigo shadow gathered under shrubs and the fringe of trees along the stream. The lily pads were thick, dark and mysterious, closed off. The pond was drawing away from him, into its own mistiness and shadow as the red light faded. It was time to go up to the house, but he lingered, saw the hillslope glow like a dying ember and the sky deepen.

The red glow touched the verandah, and flooded the room in which they ate their evening meal with dying colour, a strange, uncanny light. It had drama in it, as though the world might be burning outside, and calm, since the dying of the light was the most natural thing in the world. For Germaine the pain was so pressing that she hardly touched her food, it was as though the sun was exploding, and something inside her. She was glad of darkness coming, the growing shadows, since it hid her expression. But she had a dim apprehension that something had changed in the room, a subtle shifting of relationships.

By this time it was almost dark in the room, each of them conscious of a growing solitude coming up like a dark tide to engulf them, it was impossible to distinguish each other's features, but a curious reluctance not to disturb something made them continue to sit round the table without sending for the lamps. Conversation lapsed, becoming desultory, as shadows of leaf and cloud began to move over walls and furniture, and red light from the window gleamed back from the mirror hanging opposite, from the glassfronted cupboards, highlighting curves of silver on the table. Outside a breath of wind stirred through the branches of trees, disturbing the shadows gathering indoors, tearing off leaves, scattering petals across the gravel paths. Alice thought of the churchyard, deserted now, with night coming. Claude of the river, moving mysteriously through unknown territory hidden from him. Marthe also felt that beyond this moment lay something unknown, which made her both anxious and shy, and she was glad to sit in the shadows while Theodore talked to her stepfather, as he liked to do. She gazed at the dying flush of crimson still visible through the window and moulded a breadcrumb round and round between her finger and thumb, knowing that the children sleeping upstairs were hers now, for a time, and this was a comfort such as she had not known until now. All of them felt night coming, the tide of shadows rising as the sunset glow faded outside and the room grew dark.

On the floor above the dark had a different dimension. The children whispered and dreamed, feeling how space opened up before them, expanding in the dark under their closed eyelids. Time, the future, was endless, weighing on them. He would, he said, travel in a rocket to the moon. Perhaps you'll see my balloon, she whispered back, and fell asleep. He saw streaks of red light glow through the slats of the window shutters, and put his thumb in his mouth for comfort.

Nine o'clock, and now the reflected light from the sunset had died on the surface of the lily pond. Trees stood and submerged in shadow, a light mist gathering between their forms, clouding the outline of trunk and branch, misting over the mirror lying under the sky, which itself had begun to darken, thicken slightly, from clear blue to azure. And as it grew darker, more intense, a single star had become visible high above, as though defined by the deepening blue around it, this pinprick of pure light.

And though light still shone in the western sky, streaking the horizon with green and gold, the earth had now sunk under a sea of shadow, become part of another element, continuous with the darkening sky overhead. Nothing could halt this process, as it gradually became impossible to distinguish leaf from branch, water from rock, even the house from the hillslope behind it.

Twelve

The dark sky rises overhead, clear, the colour of night. And though it is dark several stars are reflected in the lily pond, which has become neglected, overgrown. The house lies in darkness, and nobody stands on the verandah, looking up at far more stars visible in the sky, or wanders by the pool, watching, waiting for the moon to rise. They have all gone since then. Alice first, to join her daughter in the churchyard. Much later cataracts clouded her husband's eyes, long after the war had begun and ended, guns sounded in the valley, Theodore fled with his family and returned. Nothing was ever the same again, they said, but Claude working through gunfire and silence, light and a gathering fog, watched steadfastly, saw otherwise in his lily pond. Was it yesterday, or a century ago? The stars, shining in the mirror surface of the lily pond, belie the question, since their light spans time, death and eternity.

About the Author

Eva Figes, born in Berlin, moved to England with
her family in 1939 and has lived there ever since. She
is the author of *Patriarchal Attitudes*, an important
early work in the women's movement, as well as the
highly praised novel *Waking* and a number of other
books, both nonfiction and fiction, published in England.